ISBN 978-1-7342584-8-6

KC Publications

Ojai, California

KAT DRENNAN

THE SERPENT'S COIL

A Serpent's Coil Time-Travel Historical

Book 3

KAT DRENNAN

KAT DRENNAN

THE SERPENT'S COIL

Zenobia's Spell

My beloved ones, wherever you travel in this world and the next,

these golden serpents imbued with my power

are your connection to me and to each other through eternity.

With this coil I give you power,

with these ruby eyes I give you sight,

and with the purity of this gold,

I give you life.

.

Chapter 1 - June 2019, Gaborone, Botswana

Listen

Roshana blocked out the sounds in the stuffy classroom, pinching the gold coin at the end of her necklace between her fingers and letting familiar images play in her head. Replaying her favorite visions in her brain was better than wasting time while the others struggled with a test on Shakespeare.

Granted, sometimes the visions were more like nightmares, but she knew the difference between dreams and reality. It was the message not the image she needed to pay attention to.

There was inspiration.

There was gratitude.

There was caution.

All she had to do was listen.

Roshana had finished her test half an hour ago. Shakespeare was her favorite subject. She'd sailed through the exam without having to think, not that she would ever have a need for the bard in real life.

She glanced at the clock. Only a minute had ticked by since she last looked. Ten more minutes before her real life could begin for the day.

Not that she disliked school. She was good at her studies, finishing the semester with the highest grades in her class. She just didn't see how algebra and biology would be useful once she was dancing on the stages of the world.

She let out a resigned sigh. It was better to be here than at home where her drop-out cousin, Ajani lurked like a stalker around every corner, ready to take her down for being a tag-along, *poor relative*. The hardest part was that what he said was true. She'd been raised by her aunt in Gaborone, all the way on the other side of the planet from where she was born. She had never laid eyes on her real parents, and at fifteen years old, she had resigned herself to the idea she never would.

AJ never missed a chance to rub her nose in it. "Your parents are probably on welfare somewhere, doper scumbags."

Her best friend, Shuda insisted he was just a jealous jerk. Jealous of her grades, jealous of her gorgeous long legs and beautiful smile, and jealous of the necklace her grandmother had given her.

Roshana supposed Shuda was right.

"I bet that necklace would be worth a lot of money if it was *real*," he taunted almost daily. His eyes would rake over her breasts and land on the coin at the end of the chain around her neck. She wasn't sure what he lusted after more, her body, or the gold coin. Most of the time she kept it under her shirt where no one could see it, but she never took it off.

Roshana remembered vividly the day her grandmother had popped into her life without warning and given her the necklace. In a rare moment when they were alone, her grandmother had put the necklace around her neck and told her, "Never, never, take it off. There will come a day when you'll need this coin. A now-or-never moment, do you understand?"

Roshana did not understand. She barely knew the tall woman with the natural hair and traditional clothes who dropped in unexpectedly and left without hardly saying a word. If she loved her, like grandmother's do, why didn't she take her away from her aunt and her awful cousin? Her visits always left Roshana with a hollow longing, a sense of belonging to something she couldn't touch. It made her feel like a lost soul who would never have story of her own.

One thing she did understand, though was the visions started the day she put the necklace around her neck.

Roshana had taken the coin between her fingers, felt it warm to her skin, felt a shimmering connection to something magical and strong, like holding hands with someone who knew exactly who she was. Someone who was just like her. Lost, but not alone.

From that day on, every time she held the coin and closed her eyes, that someone was there, holding her, a mirror image of herself, drinking her tears, traveling the thread of her life with her wherever she went.

Now, as the rest of the kids labored on their test, she rubbed the coin--the only physical connection she had of her former life--letting the images it invoked run loose in her head while the clock ticked slowly toward freedom.

In her vision this time, she saw a ship at sea, rocking on the swell, a group of teens were chattering excitedly over something a tall boy cradled in his palm. He looked up, caught her eye, and she was overcome with a sense of longing, and peace.

Superimposed over the entire scene were the deep red, ruby eyes of a golden serpent whose gaze was fixed on the boy as if it were watching over him. A moment later, the serpent turned its lovely golden head, and looked straight into her eyes.

The class bell's clattering ring pulled her out of her vision with a start. Kids around her were shuffling out of the classroom. She blinked a moment, the image of her vison fading fast. *No*, she thought, trying not to break the spell. She had been standing on a boat with the tall boy as a golden serpent watched over them. What was the vision trying to tell her?

But the vision was gone. In its place her aunt's words scolded in her ear. "You are an ignorant girl, Roshana; you and your silly fantasies. No one can predict the future or see into the past."

They weren't fantasies. Roshana knew all too well. It was scary how many times something she saw in one of her visions ended up actually happening. Then her aunt threatened to take her out of dance class if she didn't stop the foolishness, Roshana stopped telling her about them. Now she laughed at the thought. She couldn't stop the visions if her life depended on it.

"Roshana, let's go." Her best friend, Shuda tugged her arm. "We'll miss the bus."

Gathering her books into her backpack, Roshana dropped her test on the pile on the teacher's desk, hurried to her locker to exchange her bookbag for her dance backpack, then headed for the bus they took every day to the studio.

*   *   *

Nerves ran high as the girls gathered on the floor and at the barre in front of the mirror. Shuda pushed against Roshana's extended leg, helping her get a maximum stretch. Tomorrow was the final recital of the year. Only the top ten dancers in the troupe would be allowed to perform. The girls were anxious to show off their best talents. Roshana trembled with anticipation, dreaming that one day her dancing would be the key to getting away from Gabarone, her aunt, and her cousin. Away from everything that made her soul shudder during the night.

"Roshana Tedese!" The teacher repeated her name impatiently, pulling her out of her daydream. Roshana stood, smoothing her leotard over her hips.

Shuda hip-bumped her. "You got this, girl."

The dancers hushed as she moved into position and waited for the first plaintive guitar notes of her piece, *Speak Now*.

The music soothed her in a warm caress, spreading from her torso to her limbs, pulling at her heart strings, settling the butterflies in her stomach. Effortlessly, she bent her body like melting caramel-- fluid, then fanciful, then fraught with angst. Like a mirrored image, she danced with an invisible partner in perfect sync with her soul, lost herself in the movement, then found herself again.

Listen, listen. Speak Now.

She became the music, the words, the spirit of the dance and nothing outside that cocoon existed.

And then it was over. The cheers of the girls came to her from far away, dragging her back to reality. She had performed flawlessly and she knew it. And right after her, Shuda had done the same. They were guaranteed a position on tomorrow's team.

*   *   *

Shuda leaned in close and whispered in Roshana's ear. "Who was that lady standing off to the side of the stage? She was staring at us."

Roshana's stomach clenched with uncertainty as she peeled off her black leggings. She had seen the woman too, just before she leapt into her dance. She felt a strange jolt in her chest when their eyes had locked again as she and Shuda left the stage. "You thought that, too? I've never seen her before."

She slipped on her next outfit while she waited for the next pair to run out on stage and start their routine. She moved to the edge of the curtain and peered out. The woman was gone. Her heartbeat settled a little. There was no reason to be nervous about seeing a stranger in the crowd. Still, something in the look in the woman's eye set Roshana off balance.

Relieved, she turned to report back to Shuda and came up short with a gasp. The woman stood before her as if she'd appeared out of thin air.

"You and your partner were magnificent up there young lady. I wanted to meet you personally." The woman held out her hand. Roshana instinctively stepped back. Dance managers never let anyone backstage who didn't belong there.

"Thank you," Roshana said, hesitating. Up close, the woman was beautiful, her makeup perfection, not a hair out of place. She wore a form fitting black chemise dress with a deeply plunging neckline and three-quarter-length sleeves, her wrists jangled with gold bracelets. She was older than their dance teacher, but she carried herself well, had smooth, muscular calves. Maybe she had been a dancer in her younger years? Roshana's shoulders relaxed a bit and finally extended her hand to shake. The woman took her hand just as Shuda pirouetted in beside her.

"Oh, hello," the woman said, pulling her hand back. "And here is your lovely partner. You two ladies were wonderful. Have you been dancing together long?"

Shuda did what she always did, which was bubble over with excitement. "Since we were six," she said on a giggle. Roshana rolled her eyes.

"And what are your names?"

Roshana put her arm around Shuda's waist to stop her bouncing up and down. "I'm Roshana, and this is Shuda."

Shuda shot out her hand and shook.

The woman straightened, hooked her thumb around her purse strap. "I'm Flora." She beamed a luxurious smile. "I lead an international dance troupe and I often drop in to watch dance competitions. It's always wonderful to see young dancers like you coming up. I'll be watching your next performances. Maybe we could meet after--"

"Girls!"

Roshana flinched and turned to see her dance teacher's anxious wave, a look of concern on her face. *Uh oh.* They were about to miss their queues.

Roshana slipped her hand into Shuda's and started pulling her away. "We have to go."

CHAPTER 2 – NO CHOICE IN THE MATTER

Roshana gripped the curtain at the edge of the stage in a tight fist. As Shuda spun and leapt through her solo performance, Roshana peeked out at the crowd, her heart beating wildly beneath her ribs. The auditorium was a sea of faces; more than she had ever seen before. Was that woman, Flora from the international dance troupe out there somewhere watching? Could she really be interested in them? How amazing would that be?

As the final notes of Shuda's music built to a crescendo, Roshana's thoughts spun visions of the Palais Garnier in Paris, The Royal in London, the lofty roofs of the Sydney Opera House, the gleaming lights of Broadway. The possibilities were so tantalizing, so expansive, her chest swelled up like a balloon with the power to float her right up to the ceiling. Then the image of her AJ's snarky face popped her balloon. "The only place you'll ever get paid to dance is naked on a pole,' he'd taunted.

She let the curtain fall back into place. Anger knotted in her fists. "No," she said aloud, shaking loose her fingers. She squared her shoulders, stood tall. *He's not here, Roshana. He can't hurt you. Not here. Not now.*

The crowd applauded and whooped as Shuda sprinted off stage.

"Go get 'em 'Shana," Shuda said as she whisked by, then Roshana's music queued and she was back on stage, propelling her forward, pushing thoughts of AJ and his taunts out of her head. No way would she let his cruel words touch her on stage. Not now, not ever. The movement blocked out everything but the flow of emotion from her belly to her limbs, spinning out like satin ribbons over the crowd, up to the wings and beyond.

Ecstatic with her performance, she practically floated off stage, into the arms of her instructor. "Good job, Roshana. That was perfection."

Roshana's heart soared to the rafters as she trotted back toward the dressing room.

And then she saw her. The strange woman with the beautiful smile, heading backstage. Wow. Had she seen? What did she think?

The woman approached as Roshana touch the door. "Oh, darling girl. That was lovely."

Roshana pulled in a startled breath, some of her earlier anxiety flooding back in. International dance company? Ha. *The only place you'd get paid to dance is naked on a pole.*

The woman's eyes narrowed on her as if she could read her mind. "My, what has got you upset after such a fine performance?"

"I... nothing." She shook away the lie. Roshana sniffed. Just nerves is all. That wasn't true either. She never had to concentrate on her moves. They came naturally, like breathing. It was off stage that her doubts circled in, challenged her confidence.

Flora raised a brow. "Trouble at home?"

Roshana narrowed her eyes. "What makes you say that?" She wrapped her arms around her middle against a chill on her skin. What could this woman possibly know about her?

Flora lifted a shoulder. "It's a common reason my dancers leave home. Poverty, large family with no freedom," she cut her eyes away a moment, "... abuse--"

A bitter taste welled in the back of Roshana's throat. "That's not me," she argued. Her cousin had never abused her, right? Well, verbally was all, and the way he leered at her got under her skin; but he never actually put his hands on her.

Flora glanced down the hallway toward the stage area as if she were expecting to be interrupted. "My dancers make a good living Roshana," she said, lowering her voice. "All travel and living expenses paid, healthy food, costumes. I take very good care of my girls. Protect them." She shifted her gaze back to Roshana. "You would be a fine asset to my troupe."

Her voice had a quiet, mesmerizing quality that toyed with Roshana's senses. Travel the world with a dance troupe? The mere thought made her pulse leap in her chest. It could be the beginning of a whole new life. Then she laughed dismissively.

"My aunt would never allow it. I'm only fifteen. I'm supposed to get a proper education." That was a stretch, too. Roshana had always felt she was on borrowed time. The moment she finished school and turned eighteen, she would be turned out, on her own, that she knew.

Flora's laugh was quiet, knowing. "Several of my girls are your age." She lifted her bag from the back of her chair and slipped it over her shoulder. "You are a very lovely, talented dancer whom I would welcome anytime." She drew a card from an outside pocket of her purse and handed it to Roshana. "If you ever get to a place where you change your mind, feel free to contact me."

The bus ride back to her compound was quiet. Roshana leaned her head against the window, blind to sights outside while Shuda, exhausted from the last days' activities, snored softly, her head resting on Roshana's shoulder. She slipped Flora's card out of her pocket.

Her name was embossed over the glossy image of a deep-red rose.

Florabunda

On the back was a hand-written number and an email address. Roshana ran her thumb over the raised letters until the bus stopped at the corner by her compound, then she slipped the card into the key pocket of her leggings, stabbed her arms through the straps of her backpack, and headed up the street toward her gates.

It was as safe a place as any for people who had money. Her aunt didn't waste her time showing Roshana any personal affection or attention. Roshana had learned only recently through an overheard telephone conversation, that her aunt received a large portion of her income for Roshana's care, most of which went toward razor-wired fence tops, guard dogs at night, and plenty of fine food and clean water. Shuda's home had a dirt floor and no actual glass in the windows, none of which was a problem for Roshana. Shuda's mother was hard working and tired most of the time, but she grew the best okra in the village and treated Roshana like her own.

*   *   *

"Auntie?" Roshana called, pushing open the entry doors. There was no reply. She ghosted through the foyer to the dining room and into the main kitchen. "Auntie?" she tried again. No reply.

She pushed the swinging door and peeked into the service kitchen. No one there either. No dishes in the sink, no spicy aromas, no baked dessert cooling on the stainless-steel island. Her stomach growled, then jumped when the door swished behind her.

Her cousin stalked into the kitchen, holding a handwritten note out to her. "Looks like we're here all alone, 'Shana," he taunted, stepping into her space. His gaze raked her body, landing on her breasts, framed by her backpack's tight straps.

She covered herself with one arm and slapped the note out of his hand with the other, then turned away to read it.

Nausea gripped her stomach. Auntie and Cook had gone into town. There was leftover oxtail soup in the service fridge. *Blecckh!* She hated oxtail soup. She glanced at the clock on the stove. They wouldn't be home for another hour. She cringed, unsure which she hated most, the fact that she was expected to heat up the dreaded soup or eat by herself with her disgusting cousin. No way was she sticking around for that.

She tossed the note back to him. "You can heat up your own soup." She would slip out the back of the compound, go across the fields to Shuda's house, and stay there until Auntie got home.

When she turned to do exactly that, he plowed into her, shoving her against the wall. He circled his hands around her neck until she could barely breathe. Gasping for air, she grabbed his wrists and tried to pry him away but it was no use.

"Get away from me," she ground out behind clenched teeth. She pried at his fingers. "I'll tell Auntie!" Her mind raced. What had they taught her in women's self-defense? Knee them in the groin?

He let go of her neck and slid his hands to her wrists, pushing them over her head. "And I'll tell her you asked for it." His breath smelled like the beef jerky he always chewed.

She twisted her face away. A foot taller and sixty pounds heavier, he moved against her, a hard knot between his thighs grinding into her stomach, shoes inside her backpack crushing into her spine. Fear paralyzed her. She gasped for air.

"C'mon, little cousin. You know you want this." He pinned her wrists in one hand now, shoving the other down the front of her leggings.

"No," she cried, anger overcoming her fear. She arched her shoulders against him like her dance teacher had taught them, then slammed a knee into his groin as hard as she could. He doubled over, gripping his crotch. She cocked her knee again and aimed a fast, jabbing kick at his throat. Stunned, he fell to his side, gasping for air.

She spun away and ran as fast as she could for the mud room door. Hand on the knob, she could hear his choking cough.

He wasn't coming after her.

Not yet.

She yanked open the door and ran through the courtyard for the back of the compound where she and Shuda had a secret hole in the fence behind rows of dried corn in the vegetable garden. Thank goodness this happened in the daytime. If it was night, the dogs would be loose in the yard and they weren't choosy about whose behind they grabbed hold of. Throwing a last glance over her shoulder to make sure she wasn't followed, she prized open the break in the chain link fence, took off her backpack and pushed her body through, then pulled her pack through behind her.

She crouched low as she ran between the green hedge and her neighbor's razor-wire-topped fence until she reached the bus stop, then slipped her pack over her shoulders and jogged toward the little row of plastered block houses where Shuda lived. She skirted the side of Shuda's house, moved a plastic bucket under the window, hoisted herself up, and rapped her knuckles on the window frame. "Shuda!"

A moment later, her friend appeared, her littlest brother on her hip.

"Roshana? Oh my god, what's happened? What's wrong?"

"Can I use you phone?"

"Of course, but why? You look awful."

Roshana looked frantically over her shoulder, then back at her friend. "Just let me in, okay? I'll tell you everything."

Shuda met her at the back door and showed her through to the kitchen, where three more of her siblings played on the floor with a batch of kittens.

Roshana lowered her pack to the table and caught her breath, told Shuda everything that had happened, then slipped Flora's card out of her leggings pocket.

Shuda put down her brother and took the card, shaking her head. "You can't just go with her. We don't even know who she is. Not really."

Roshana shrugged. "Maybe. But I know who my cousin is for sure. If I stay, he will ruin me. Ruin everything."

"But how do you know Flora is what she says?"

"I don't."

"But--"

Roshana thought about her cousin, writhing in pain on their service kitchen floor. If she told Auntie what happened, who would she believe? She knew the answer to that question. "I have no choice. Please. Get me your phone."

Chapter 3 – A Now-or-Never Moment

Only ten minutes had passed since Roshana made the call when the limousine arrived. The girls glanced from Shuda's porch across her okra patch to see the car come to a stop on the oiled dirt road in front of her house.

Roshana's heart shrank to a tiny, cold fist inside her ribcage. She was more frightened now than when AJ had held her against the wall. What she was about to do would change her life forever and she had no way of knowing if that were a good thing or a bad.

The door to the limousine opened. Shuda touched her shoulder from behind. "'Shana?"

"I have to, Shuda." The words made her throat ache with regret. "I told you what happened."

"But--"

"I'm sorry," she whispered, and stepped off the porch.

*　　*　　*

"Hello Roshana." Miss Flora's voice, honeyed and welcoming made Roshana think of the old fairy tales. The old hag offers a sweet apple to the young maiden...

But Flora wasn't an old hag. She was older than their dance teacher, but younger than her aunt. She could have been a dancer once, because she was lithe and beautiful. She had the carriage, the grace, the confidence.

Now, Flora scooted across the back seat, making room for Roshana to sit next to her. Roshana sat tentatively, leaving the limousine door open.

"Do you want to tell me about it?" Flora asked, one eyebrow raised.

Roshana shook her head. "I... I just changed my mind is all."

The truth. But not the whole truth. No way could she say the words. Nausea threatened at the memory of being at her cousin's mercy, his fingers clawing at her, holding her against the wall, pressing himself against her.

Flora looked her up and down, taking note of Roshana's attire. She was still in her dance clothes-- leggings and a tank, her dance backpack slung over her shoulder. Then her gaze went deeper, as if she could see into Roshana's soul. Her smile turned down at the corners, then she nodded her head. Roshana glanced up to see Shuda was still watching from her front porch.

Flora cleared her throat. "Close the door a moment, Roshana."

"Close the door?" Anxiety jittered across her shoulders. This was a mistake. Every nerve in her body told her so. She reached out a hand to grab the door handle but didn't draw it closed. Miss Flora was a stranger, but honestly, she was the only one who had offered any hope. Her Aunt wouldn't protect her. She would hear no complaints about her son's behavior. Never had. And her grandmother? She couldn't remember the last time she'd seen her.

Flora's smile softened into the one Roshana remembered from earlier at the dance studio. She rested her hands on the leather handbag in her lap. Roshana's gaze landed on a heavy ring on Flora's pointer finger that looked like a large drop of blood gripped in gold talons.

Uncertainty gathered at the back of her throat. She forced herself to look away.

"Roshana, I know you are a big girl and can probably take care of whatever is happening at home," Flora said. "You're strong and I believe you will get away on your own... eventually."

Roshana nodded, her eyes fixed on her own hands. After what happened today, she wasn't so sure. Even now, in the relative safety of the fancy limousine, she could feel her cousin's fingers digging at her, prying into her most private places.

Flora tapped her on her thigh, that gaudy ring bobbing on her finger. "Roshana, look at me."

Roshana looked up slowly. Flora's eyes caught hers and held them with a determined look. "You see, the thing is, Roshana. You were lucky to catch me at all. I'm on my way out of town right now and I'm not coming back."

Roshana sucked in her breath, her hopes for another chance started to evaporate. "Not coming back?"

"Like I said, we're starting an international tour. We fly out of Johannesburg tomorrow, to Paris, then on to the United States."

The United States? Roshana's heart did a little pirouette. Dare she dream such a thing? She squeezed her hands tight in her lap, her teeth biting hard into her bottom lip, willing her heartbeat to settle. "Tomorrow?"

She lifted her gaze to the porch. Shuda was still standing there, her face a mask of dread.

Flora reached out her finger and gently turned her face back, lifting her chin until they were eye-to-eye.

Roshana swallowed hard.

"If you want to come with us, you must leave now. Understand?"

"Now? You mean right this minute?"

Flora's eyes hardened. All tenderness and understanding had gone out of them. Instead Roshana saw a shrewd businesswoman who had no time for indecisive young girls.

Flora checked her watch. "All plans are already in place. If we don't leave this minute we'll miss our flight to Johannesburg, and I can't do that to the rest of the troupe."

"But what about my Aunt? My clothes? School?"

Flora's unblinking gaze made Roshana's stomach clench. For a moment, she longed to be anywhere but here in this car with a woman she hardly knew. A last glance out the window to see Shuda's face said it all. She was frightened for her, wanted her to get out of the car.

Roshana knew for sure, if she left now, she would probably never see her best friend again. But staying meant going back to her aunt's house and her cousin. She couldn't bear the thought of his hands on her again.

Flora's gentle smile returned, as if she were reading Roshana's mind. This woman had seen the world. Seen through Roshana's brave front. Seen her fear.

Roshana lifted her hand to her throat feeling suddenly more alone than she had ever felt in her life. She never wanted to face her cousin again, but leave? Now? All by herself? With nothing but the clothes on her back and her dancing shoes? She gripped the gold coin in her fingers. In an instant, an electric certainty flooded her like a dam had broken somewhere in her chest and flowed through her entire body: This was one of those *now-or-never* moments her grandmother had told her about.

She let go of the coin and turned to face Flora. "I don't have any clothes except what I've got on..."

Flora's grin widened. "Have you been to the airport in Johannesburg?"

Her grandmother had brought her into the country from the States, so yes, she had probably been there but, "Not since I was old enough to remember."

"Heaps of shops there," Flora said, tapping on the window to alert the driver they were leaving. "We can grab you a change of clothes there," she hesitated, taking in Roshana's worn jogging shoes, muddy from traipsing through Shuda's okra patch, "and a pair of shoes. Then we'll meet up with the rest of the girls and fill out your wardrobe in Paris."

Shopping? In Paris? Then on to the United States? Suddenly Roshana could not get enough air. A smile spread wider on her lips than she imagined was possible. She pulled the door closed on every warning, every regret, everything she had ever known. She gripped the gold coin again. *What have I got to lose?*

CHAPTER 4 – JAMAL BREAKS HIS PROMISE

Newport Beach, California, 2019

Jamal slipped on a sandal, glancing up just in time to see Rags drag the other one out the door, dangling between his legs like prized prey.

"Hey, you little stinker!" The cat was annoying as hell but he was also one of Jamal's favorite things about spending the night in the guest room at Lexi's house on Balboa Island. One minute the huge ginger tabby would be curled up purring in his lap while he did his homework, the next he was stealing Jamal's pen for a game of hide and seek.

Anxious to meet his friends for an early morning run down to San Onofre, Jamal thumped down the stairs, hitting the last step in time to see the cat plow through the swinging cat door, sandal in tow.

It was Saturday, and Jamal had been looking forward to a little free time with his new friends, home school almost behind him and the summer stretching ahead like a dream; a big change from being stuck in the compound at Bole or confined to the decks of his father's research vessel.

His relationship with his father had undergone a transition over the last year. It wasn't that long ago that Jamal believed his young father, Zaire, was his big brother; that his parents had adopted him as an infant. But when his "father" passed away a few years back, his "mother" told him the truth. The loving couple who had raised him were actually his grandparents. Since Zaire spent most of his time traveling the world's oceans looking for treasure, Jamal rarely saw his biological father, let alone spent any time with him.

Despite the fact that his paternal grandmother had come clean, Jamal's life hadn't changed much until she passed away a little over a year ago. Jamal and Zaire were thrown together of necessity, a development that took some getting used to and begged another question: If the person he believed all his life was his brother was actually his father, then who was his mother? And where was she?

Fortified with little more than a hunch and a cryptic message from an old woman he'd never seen before who'd showed up unannounced at their compound in Bole, Jamal had pressured Zaire to let him try and locate his biological mom, Alexis Hill.

What he soon learned was that Alexis came with her own cobbled-together family, including Tessa Madigan-Koenig, and her private detective husband, Phillip. The rest was, as they say, history.

Since relocating to the US while Zaire launched a new destination resort in Carlsbad, for the first time in his young life, Jamal had personal freedom enough to actually breathe.

"C'mon, Rags," he begged impatiently as the cat's feather-duster tail disappeared into the next-door neighbor, Tessa's garage. A moment later Jamal stood at the door of the infamous forbidden workshop.

He hadn't been privy to all that went on with Tessa and Lexi and the jewelry they'd discovered in Tessa's old house. The adults had held those cards close to their chests. All he knew was that a woman had been killed right in this very house because of it, and Lexi and his dad had had their own supernatural adventure under what he imagined was the spell of the Serpent's Coil bracelet. If you asked him, they were all being a bit dramatic about the whole thing. The secrecy was more likely to do with an investigation still going on over Cauldron Industry's involvement in antiquities theft.

Rags meowed impatiently from behind the door. Jamal peeked inside. The cat leaped to a cubby hole and curled up, leaving Jamal's leather flip-flop on the floor. He pressed his hand flat against the door. Surely, it was okay to slip in and get his shoe. He could care less about some old bracelet.

He pushed open the door a little further. Rags stretched his back in a high arch, toes spread, claws extended, then batted his paw at something in the cubby. Light angling through the front casement window caught on a golden flash as that something fell to the floor, rolled on its edge toward his shoe, then wobbled in a circle a moment before it finally settled against it. Ruby red eyes glinted in the head of the snake bracelet and seemed to stare directly at him.

There you are my love.

A prickly frisson slithered up the back of Jamal's neck along with velvety words that coiled around his psyche. Tessa, he thought. Everyone else had left for the day. She had probably heard a noise down here from upstairs and come to investigate.

He glanced over his shoulder.

No one there.

He pulled in a deep breath and let it out.

Just get the damn shoe, fool, he told himself. *One step in, snag the sandal, and get out of there in a flash and no one will be the wiser.* He sucked in another breath, shifted his weight forward and let the momentum carry him across the threshold.

Rags leapt down from the cubby and strolled over, running his silky body across the back of Jamal's legs. He relaxed and reached out to grab his shoe, then froze. In a slow motion like in the movies, the golden snake uncoiled and slithered to wrap itself around the strap of the sandal.

No way. That just...couldn't...

His heart thumped hard in his chest. He crouched, gripping his knees, then startled at thumping sounds overhead. He looked up at the wood plank ceiling. Rhythmic footsteps thudded above, along with the hum of a vacuum cleaner. Relieved, he let out his breath. Tessa upstairs cleaning. *Everything is okay, just get the effing shoe and get out of here.*

But when he looked back, the snake was staring at him. *Staring. At. Him.* Captivated, he reached out a trembling finger and touched its nose. In a flash of golden light, the snake uncoiled, raced up his arm and settled around his biceps, searing heat into his skin. *Oh no, that's heaps of no good.*

Then three things happened simultaneously. His mouth went dry, his knees went liquid, and he slid down, flat on his back.

*   *   *

Jamal was blinking at light seeping in through tiny oblong windows when he realized everything had changed. The wind had definitely been knocked out of him, but he couldn't remember how, or even *if* that's what happened.

Where the heck was he?

He was definitely on a boat and a big one, like his father's vessel, the *Salacia.* Substantial. Oceangoing. He could tell by the way it sat solid in the water. But unlike his father's vessel, outfitted for exploration, this one was fancy, like the party boats owned by some of his father's partners and friends. How in the heck had he gotten here?

His head felt over-sized, vacant. It must be a dream.

He started to get up. Then his gaze fell on a smear of dark red on the woodwork of a large cushion next to the one where he lay. He sat up straight, rubbed his eyes. Filtered light framed another smudge on the carpeted floor. He stood, stepped across the narrow space, and touched the smear with a finger. The edges of it were dry, but the center of the smudge—a thick blob of deep, dark red--hadn't yet dried. He stared at it a moment, then brought it to his nose and sniffed. The unmistakable coppery odor of blood.

Jarred, he grabbed the coin necklace at his neck and fell back on the cushion. In a sickening flash he saw it. Saw her. A young woman--blond, head hanging limp, mouth askew, hair streaming almost to the floor--was being carried from the berth.

He sat up slowly. It was just like before in Tessa's workshop. He'd touched the bracelet and the necklace and been transported… somewhere else. But this time, his sense of purpose was urgent. He'd seen this place before. It was the vision he'd had when he'd seen his sister. Sleek, muscular legs, skin a few shades lighter brown than his own, springy curls gathered in two knots atop her head: a straight, slender nose, sharp jawline, and green eyes like his own.

Certainty flitted around in his chest a moment before it settled low in his belly. *Sister.* He leaned against the bed, gripping the coin in one hand, and resting the other on the cushion, his fingers spread like sensors over the surface. She'd been here. Right here in this very space. He knew it. Felt it in the deepest part of his soul. But where was here? And if she had been here, had she witnessed what he'd just seen? Where was she now?

*　　*　　*

"Jamal!"

He startled, jumping nearly out of his skin. Eyes flying wide, the light beaming in Tessa's workshop windows momentarily blinded him. He shielded them with a hand at his brow and squinted in the direction of the voice.

She stood in the doorway and she was not smiling. *Uh oh.*

"Tessa," he started in, apologetically. His dad and Lexi would be disappointed in him, but he felt worse about Tessa catching him in the act. He had invaded her space and the disappointment on her face stung him sharply.

"What are you doing in here?"

"Um." He stood on wobbly legs, rubbed at a raw spot on his arm. "Uh, Rags. He took my sandal?" His words sounded so lame, like he was trying out a version of the truth. He twisted around. The sandal lay on the floor. Rags was nowhere in sight. The snake bracelet was on the cubby shelf where it started, an inanimate object with ruby eyes that now looked flat and lifeless.

Tessa crossed her arms over her chest, her gaze going to the spot he rubbed on his arm. She strode in, gently pried his fingers away. "So, where did you go?"

"Go?"

She huffed out a heavy sigh, leaned against the workbench. "You forget who you're talking to. I know what happened here, Jamal, so don't try to woof me."

He slumped onto the day bed opposite her, feeling like a jerk. "I didn't mean to touch it, honestly, Tessa. I just--"

She held up her hand to stop him. "Neither did I or your mother. That's the way it happens. That's why we didn't want you down here at all."

Still shaken from what he had seen and the sense his sister was in some kind of trouble, he studied Tessa's face. She didn't look angry. She looked concerned. And she was Lexi's best friend. He could trust her. Hopefully. Had to trust someone if he were to actually help his sister. Worry crept into his heart on cold little feet.

Tessa moved to the day bed, put her arm around his shoulder. "Jamal?"

"I didn't go to no ancient bath or coliseum if that's what you mean."

"Oh?"

"But I did go... *somewhere*." He rubbed at his arm a moment. When it stung, he pulled his hand away. Made his decision. Whatever trouble he might be in for coming down here when he wasn't supposed to couldn't be much compared to the feeling he got when he felt his sister. The image of the young woman's hair dragging over the floor played in his memory. His sister's trouble was the kind that put you in danger. Got you killed.

"Um. It wasn't the first time," he admitted. Relief swept over him in little waves, releasing some of the tension in his gut. He told her about the first time he felt his sister, when he'd been holding on to his gold coin.

"I didn't actually see anything that time, only felt her panic, her fear." His face felt suddenly sweaty and hot. "But this time, just now..." he glanced up at the bracelet. "I touched the bracelet when I reached for my shoe, and..." The memory of how fast the little gold snake slithered up his arm made him shudder. "This time, I saw a *place*. I could feel she'd been there, but she wasn't there with me." He lowered his gaze to his hands, threaded his fingers and squeezed until his knuckles hurt. "I saw blood. On the bed, on the floor..."

Tessa stared at him now, interested. "Do you have any idea where you were?"

He shook his head. "The only thing I know for sure is that it was in the *now*. The cabin had all the modern stuff, like a flat screen and a wet bar, and..." He scratched his forehead a moment. "I thought that bracelet took you *back* in time."

"We don't know what the rules are, Jamal. That's why we didn't want you involved; but from what you just told me, and what you told us all before, you're already involved." She looked away a moment, blew out a long breath, and turned back. "And, if--this is a big if, mind you--you are seeing something happening in the present and your sister is involved--"

"We might be able to help her."

Tessa nodded.

"So, I guess we have to tell my dad."

"You guess right. And Lexi and Phillip. Anything you can remember of what you saw that might give us a clue where to start."

"So you believe me? That I could really be feeling my sister?"

She gave him a hard hug. "Again, you forget who you're talking to. I'd believe almost anything you told me connected to that damn bracelet."

Chapter 5 – First Class Ticket to Ride

Gateway to Paris

Inside the first-class cabin, lights came up from a twilight blue to a warm morning glow and the Air France theme music slowly got louder. A flight attendant brought Roshana a warm face cloth and a packet with tooth paste and a toothbrush, along with a breakfast menu.

She smiled, sleepy-eyed, as the attendant made her way quietly through the first-class cabin. The last two days had been a blur. One day, her cousin had nearly raped her in her aunt's service kitchen, the next she was given a new name and passport and whisked away leaving Gaborone forever.

Flora had made good on her promise at Johannesburg International Airport, buying her the coolest jeans she had ever laid eyes on, along with a white silk shirt, a pair of rhinestone studded espadrilles, an Hermes scarf, and a pair of huge silver hoop earrings that hung halfway to her shoulders. Her aunt would have scoffed at the pretense of it all, but Roshana beamed, leaving her old clothes in the waste basket in the airport ladies room. The outfit made her look years older than fifteen and not only that, like she'd just stepped off a Paris runway.

She studied the menu. *Spinach quiche or croissant?* She let go a quiet laugh. She'd been lucky to get a bite out of a piece of stale toast at her aunt's house before AJ clamored into the kitchen, grabbed it out of her hands, and gobbled it down.

Her stomach rumbled. She sat up in her seat, pushed the button to bring it up from sleep position, where she could see over the top of the privacy barrier. Flora still slept, a silk tiger print shade covering her eyes.

She marked both the quiche and the pudding on the menu card, along with a fruit bowl and a champagne, just to see what would happen.

When the flight attendant returned, she checked the menu and shook her head at the champagne. Well, it was worth a try.

"And, oh, I nearly forgot," the attendant went on. "I'll need your paperwork completed before we land in Paris."

Roshana nodded, her eyes glancing to the pocket behind the seat in front of her. "Of course."

Sliding her tray over her lap, she studied the paperwork again. She was still a little nervous about the information on her new passport. Flora had taken her to a private home in Gaborone where the fellow shot her picture, took her thumb print, and went to work while Flora explained.

"It's important you travel with me as an eighteen-year-old. It just saves me a lot of hassle when we pass through different countries."

That was okay. In fact, it was pretty cool. The hard part—the part that didn't sit right—was Flora wanted her to change her name as well. "Wouldn't that be--" *illegal*, she was going to say.

But Flora was up pacing, pinching her bottom lip between her fingers. "Something snappy, exotic, worldly, original."

Roshana had never liked her name. It was like it had been tacked on at the last minute by somebody who didn't care whether it fit. Not anything like her friends at school. A mistaken identity. She didn't even know who had given it to her. Roshana had gripped her necklace then, the only thing she had of the person she had been before. The new name came to her on a whisper in the back of her mind: *Zenobia*. The ancient queen she'd learned about in her history class.

She sat up a little straighter. "But won't they want my birth certificate or something?"

Flora laughed. "Oh, honey. Of course they will. It's included in the package."

Roshana's fingers had trembled as she wrote her new name down for the first time: *Zenobia*.

Flora had tapped the paper in front of her. "Okay. We need a last name. One syllable, to counter the three syllable first name."

"Page," Roshana said. Like turning a page on a new life.

"Zenobia Page," Flora repeated, floating her hands in front of her, like a dancer in a *plié*. "I like it. It's got rhythm. Flow."

She was right. It did have a nice ring to it. Some of Roshana's uncertainty melted away. "And I'll be Zoey Page most of the time, okay?"

Flora had nodded agreement and tapped the Last Name space of the paper. "Write it down. You'll be Zoey Page from now on."

Now, with her new passport and the travel documents before her, Roshana was having second thoughts. What if someone went looking for Roshana Tesede? There would be no record of her leaving the country or entering another one. It would be just like she had disappeared that day in Gaborone when she handed her passport to the gate clerk and got on the tiny plane for Johannesburg. Then she heaved up a heavy sigh. What difference did it actually make? She was never going back. Ever.

The flight attendant returned with her breakfast and orange juice in a tall, fluted glass. Roshana handed her the forms. The attendant skimmed over them, then smiled back at her. "Zenobia Page. What an unusual name."

Roshana sipped the juice, imagining a real Bellini tickling the back of her throat and in that moment, she vowed never to think of herself as Roshana Tesede again. "Zenobia, after the queen. But my friends call me Zoey."

Zoey gasped at the orchid-draped lobby of the *Hotel George Cinque* while Flora ordered their luggage brought up to their suites. From the moment she'd seen the Eiffel Tower on the plane's video camera, the final remnants of her former life cracked and peeled away like a snake shedding its skin. They were in Paris! For reals.

She spun a circle, taking it all in.

Flora pushed her toward the elevators. "Come on. My assistant has already checked us in. Two of the girls are in the suite waiting for us."

Zoey's stomach quivered with excitement. This was truly a dream. She doubted her namesake, the ancient Queen, ever experienced the luxury laid out before her now.

They entered Flora's suite first where Chantal, Flora's assistant, waited. Her eyes went directly to Zoey, sweeping over her like she was a fancy dessert. "Oh my." She lifted Zoey's hands and spun her around. "Miss Flora said you were exceptional, but I had no idea."

Flora gave her an impatient push in the direction of the double doors leading to the adjoining suite. "Hush now. We don't want her to get a big head."

They opened the doors to bright squeals of delight. A petite girl about Zoey's age with alabaster skin, dark red curls grazing her shoulders, and eyes the deep green of the Chobe River rushed to embrace her.

"I'm so happy you're here! Chantal said you might join us for our shopping trip. I can't wait, can you? I'm Fiona. What was your name? Zenobia?"

The girl's enthusiasm, and a light sprinkling of freckles across her nose, reminded Zoey of Shuda, with a tiny pang of regret. "Just, Zoey is fine," she said, returning the hug. *Zoey Page.*

Her gaze shifted to take in the other girl. She was nearly as tall as Zoey, with a willowy frame, and wheat-colored hair swept back from her face in a high ponytail that spilled over her shoulder nearly to her waist. Her eyes were a striking, tropical blue. Her expression--sullen and secretive--was one Zoey recognized all too well. She was a competitor. A presence to be reckoned with on stage and off. But there was something else there, something Zoey recognized, and that recognition sent a shiver up the back of her neck and made her cringe.

She gave the tall girl a tentative smile, and for a moment, their eyes held. Then the other girl broke the connection, turned, and strode to the bathroom, shutting the door behind her.

Fiona looped her arm through Zoey's and turned her toward the bedrooms, lifting herself up a bit to whisper into her ear. "That's Victoria. I don't know what's got into her. She's usually sweet and friendly. She's been with the troupe the longest."

"Oh? How long is that?"

Fiona shrugged. "A month? Maybe two? The troupe did a performance in London just before I joined up."

She led her into an expansive bedroom where two silk canopied beds draped in blue satin duvets and covered with matching pillows graced opposite walls. An elegant violet velvet sofa commanded the center of the room, offering a view of the city that included the Eiffel Tower in the near distance.

Zoey's chest expanded until she felt lighter than air. Her bag had been deposited next to the sofa. Fiona nudged her to the balcony. "Don't worry, that couch opens to a super comfortable bed. I slept there last night when Chantal was here with us.

Zoey drifted her fingers across the gilded frame of what she thought might be an actual Louis XV chair, then literally floated to the balcony. She gripped the ornate railing and gazed out over the rooftops of what she always thought would be the most beautiful city in the world. The view did not disappoint.

"I thought there would be more girls. Flora said a troupe, so--"

"Oh, there are ten of us. Victoria and I earned the chance to go shopping with Flora at our dance practice yesterday. The rest of the girls are staying in a hostel on the left bank, close to the Sorbonne. Flora rented us a practice studio near there."

Zoey's chest deflated a little. No doubt, she would be staying in the hostel tomorrow night. Then she realized a hostel in Paris was likely better than any place she'd find in Gaborone on her own.

"We'll be rehearsing there for a few more days," Fiona went on, excitedly, "then on to the US."

The United States in a few days? Incredible! "Where in the US?"

"I don't really know," Fiona said. "This is my first trip, just like you. I was at a recital in Dublin when I met Flora." Her gaze went distant, a hint of strain at the corners of her eyes, then a shine that Zoey thought might have turned to a tear if she hadn't swept it away with the back of her hand.

"So, you miss your parents then?" Zoey asked.

"Parents? Ha." Fiona ran her fingers through her curls. "Believe me when I say, Zoey. I'm better off here."

The two of them gazed out over the city for a long, silent moment.

"Me, too," Zoey said at last. *Me too.*

"Zenobia's not your real name, though, right?"

Zoe looked at Fiona now, the afternoon sun shining through flyaway curls framed her head in a reddish halo.

"No," she said on a chuckle. "She was a queen in the third century." She lifted her hand to her necklace a moment, drawing insight from it. "She defied the Roman emperor and ruled all of Palmyra for a time, that would be near Syria now. She was a warrior queen. Gave them a run for their money back in the day."

Fiona stared at her, drawn in. "My, aren't we the history buff."

Zoey grinned back. "My favorite subject, after Shakespeare. My real name is Zoey."

Fiona stared at her a moment longer, as if she were testing the truth of her confession, then turned back to view the city. "My real name is Coralee Byrne. Flora thought it was too Irish. Can't say as I blame her. So when she suggested Fiona, I snapped it up. Fiona Reed. It fits, doesn't it?" She did a perfect pirouette.

Zoey laughed. "Yup. It does. How old are you, really?"

Again, the long stare. "Well, I'm not eighteen, if that's what you're thinking."

"I'm fifteen," Zoe confessed, the image of Victoria's enigmatic stare played across the back of mind. Fiona admitted she came from a bad family environment, and so had she. Judging by the pain she recognized in Victoria's eyes, the three of them had that in common.

Gazing at the romantic icon in the distance, she wondered how a dance troupe made up of young, virtually amateur dancers afforded Flora first class transportation, double suites at the Henry Cinque, and passage to America for ten young women. Until this moment she had been so taken in by the shining opportunity, the luxury, the shopping, and the fancy suite she hadn't given the rest of it much thought at all. But the look she saw in Victoria's eyes--the one who'd been with Fiona the longest--took some of the shine off of it. They were staying in a luxury hotel and about to go shopping on the *Champs Elysses*. So why did the willowy blond look so despondent?

The question caught in Zoey's throat and stuck there like stone. She was only fifteen and didn't know much about the world outside Gaborone, but she wasn't stupid. As much as she wanted to believe in this rosy, *Florabunda* world, she sensed an underlying tension she couldn't ignore.

Zenobia stood on the diaz of her villa in Tibur, chin lifted in defiant reverie as a light breeze played with the silk draped around her ankles. Marble columns framed a circular moat around a domed retreat, shaded by palms and cooled by the breath of the mountains. It was a welcome change from the heat that would be stifling her beloved Antioch this time of year. Aurelian had been generous to provide her a villa fit for a warrior queen to live in after her defeat in Palmyra.

She squared her shoulders. The new villa was comfortable, but nothing like the grandeur of her palace at home. She deserved better, after all she'd suffered since her husband and son had been assassinated. She was descended from the Ptolemies and Cleopatra, after all. It was a story handed down about her that had served her well. No one knew who her father truly was, and her mother was long beyond asking.

It had been nearly three months since she last looked out over the beloved rooftops of Antioch, a city that since her husband's demise, she had turned into a cultural oasis of learning and the arts. Wrists shackled in chains, she had stood on the sweeping steps of her palace and stitched the image of the sun's fire on the spires of her palace in the golden cloth of her memory, knowing as they dragged her away, she would never see that fire again.

Now, not one to be put down, she pressed her lips tight against the urge to weep.

She was homesick.

She was tired.

She had suffered crushing defeat.

But though the warrior queen had retreated deep inside her, she was still there, and Zenobia would be damned if she let anyone forget it.

Word of her capture had spread throughout the land, and despite her defeat, powerful men petitioned for audience with her. They wanted to see for themselves this aberration--a warrior queen fit to topple the Roman armies. They sought to garner for themselves some of the power she must surely still command.

They came, they waited, and were mostly turned away.

Cyrus, the Praetorian guard assigned to transport her from Antioch to Rome in chains, remained on duty at the villa, day after day, the stalwart champion of her beleaguered soul.

He moved in close now, close enough for her to breathe in the heady, cardamom scent of his body.

"What troubles you this morning, my Queen?" he asked, his voice a low rumble near her ear.

Queen? She rested her hand on her belly, then sent him a mock querulous look. "Why do you insist on calling me your queen? I am no such thing to you, even though I was to my people not so long ago."

"I beg your pardon, Zenobia." He bent low, taking off his shining metal helmet. His muted laugh was at once annoying and irresistible. Not since her husband had been assassinated, had she had any interest in a man, other than to slice his head off in battle. But Cyrus had a way of reminding her she was not just a defeated warrior queen, but a beautiful and still desirable woman.

She turned to face him, pressed her hand against his chest, the gold bands at her wrist jingling heavily. "You were a soldier. Do you not chafe under this household duty when you could be out conquering territory under the Emperor's command?"

"So, it is boredom that stalks you, is it? Is the countryside too peaceful for the warrior queen?" He lifted his hand to indicate the hills outside the compound. "A veritable respite from all the strife in the city? Gilded bedposts? Glass urns, running water, private baths?"

The corners of his mouth quirked up and she let out a slow breath. They had shared all those luxuries together and then some. Just the thought of those things, and the low rumble of his voice sent warmth through her belly. "A gilded cage is still a prison, even if it does have a handsome jailer."

She pushed past him into the garden where lilies floated in the shallow moat.

He moved closer, placed his helmet on the wide railing and joined her in the morning shade. She swallowed hard at his proximity. Though she had much experience with men in her life, most of it had been calculated as a way to gain or maintain power, not through any compelling physical attraction. Now she was in a different place. She had nothing to gain or lose. Nothing to calculate or command. Inside this prison, she was free to indulge her innermost desires and inadvertently, or perhaps, intentionally, Aurelian had supplied her with the perfect jailer. A willing partner to while away the hours.

She had no business encouraging this Praetorian Guard. Not only should he have been off limits by his rank and loyalty to Rome, but by the deep walnut color of his skin, his sharp jaw and cheekbones, and his tall frame, he was clearly not even Roman. Yet, she was powerless to stop herself. With two grown sons, one assassinated and the other lost who knew where, she had no one in this world to confide in but this man.

He reached out and toyed with one of the tight braids looping near her ear. "By some accounts, you have been lucky to keep your elegant head, let alone be housed in luxury by your conqueror."

She stepped away. He was teasing her now, and she had to admit, she craved his attention. She rarely had visitors. There had been weeks when he was the only person she had talked to other than her woman's servants and the cook. "By whose account?"

"Well. Aurelian was none too delighted when he heard you had dragged his look alike through Antioch in chains, claiming victory at your hands. He might have had you executed for that alone."

She had, after all, defied Rome and taken all of Syria, Lebanon, and had her sights on Alexandria while Emperors focused on other territories as if her beloved Palmyra meant nothing to the empire.

He moved in behind her now, ran his hands over her shoulders and let them come to rest on her belly. She covered his hands with her own. "Ah, but it was the coins that tipped him over the edge," he said.

"The coins indeed," she returned. "What self-respecting emperor would stand by and have his likeness stricken from the tender of the land and replaced by the image of a woman?"

"Self-respecting? I wonder." He pressed a kiss to the top of her head. "But reminding you of your blessings is not why I came to you this morning."

His voice was solemn now, tinged with a hint of regret.

She turned out of his embrace and leaned against the balustrade, adjusting the wide, bejeweled belt at her hips. "Oh? And what is that?"

"The senator from Thrace, Gaius Carus, has sent word of his return. He wishes audience with you ... again." Judging by the disdain she saw pinched around his jawline, Cyrus was none too thrilled to deliver the message. They had shared great intimacy since the senator had first called, the day she'd arrived at the villa, and though they hadn't spoken of it, each knew there was no future in their union.

Zenobia drew in a breath, attempting to ease the sudden ache in her heart. She shifted her gaze into the distance. On his visit, the honorable senator had praised her efforts to secure Palmyra under her control. "Aurelian squanders a great asset keeping you a prisoner here," he'd told her, clearly trying to flatter.

Indeed, word across the empire was that the only way a woman could have gotten away with all she had done until her capture was that she had the strength and courage of a man and the magic of a sorceress. The senator had wanted to see for himself what all the fuss was about.

"Is it true," he'd pressed her, "That you possess supernatural powers to support your cause?"

She remembered clearly that day with a modicum of pride. "If possessing the will greater than the Emperor's to protect the economic interests in Rome's far-reaching provinces is considered supernatural, then I will admit to having that power on my side. That is not to say that I have the will to support another's agenda. What I did was done in the interest of preserving Palmyra, not the Empire."

The portly man had advanced on her then, taking both her hands in his. "As my wife, Zenobia, you would have the freedom and wealth to continue your efforts in cultural education as you wish. We would make a powerful team, you and I."

Ambition had glinted in his eyes. The heavy gold collar around his neck, and thick gold cuffs at his wrists signified his position near the Emperor's inner circle. Ambition and avarice were easily identified in the governing classes. She was no admirer of either. She had bid him let her consider his offer for a time and sent him away like the others who followed.

Now that the prospect of spending the rest of her days isolated from the empire loomed large before her, the senator's proposition was more attractive. A woman accustomed to running an empire isn't easily locked away. Not to mention the life she felt growing in her belly, an unintended consequence of spending time alone with Cyrus. It wouldn't be long before there would no concealing the fact that their activities had extended beyond what some would consider appropriate for jailer and prisoner.

Marriage to a respected senator would be of mutual benefit. Once the deed was done it would be little matter that the child would likely have darker skin than either of its parents. By the time it was born, she would have made herself indispensable to the senator and at his age, fathering a child would attest to his power. Then again, there was the possibility he would reject her and the child outright the moment he realized the offspring could not possibly be his own.

Cyrus stared at her now, surely reading every thought in her head. Maybe the best thing for her and this child would be to run away with him to wherever he had come from and turn her back on the grandeur of Rome.

She wished to the gods she could call on her old oracle, Shahira from Palmyra. Her shoulders drooped at the thought. She'd only half believed in all that supernatural fuss. Shahira hadn't foreseen the assassination of her husband, after all. Zenobia had seen *that* in the future all by herself.

She turned her back to Cyrus now, taking in the long view toward the mountains and faraway Thrace. Whatever was on the horizon for her, she knew with one hundred percent certainty, her future would not hold any power stuck here in this villa alone.

Without turning around and pressing a hand to her chest at a sharp ache in her heart, she said "Send word I will see him." She didn't want to see the look on Cyrus's face when he heard the words.

*　　　*　　　*

Five years later. Thrace, Roman Empire, 279 CE

Gaius Carus was a quaestor appointed by Aurelian, which was to say, a high-ranking senator who carried out the will of the Emperor on all matters financial in his province. In exchange, he was able to maintain his household in splendid luxury. Twenty years Zenobia's senior and in questionable health, Gaius valued her assistance in carrying out his duties, something his age might otherwise have excluded him from the emperor's service. While living with Gaius held much to be desired compared to the days spent with Cyrus, life at his home in Thrace was preferable to spending the rest of her days as a prisoner in Rome.

Six months after their nuptials and subsequent relocation to Thrace, Zenobia had given birth to twins. It was abundantly clear that Gaius could not have been the father. To her utter delight and Gaius' less-than-surprised acceptance, the healthy baby boy and girl bore a sound resemblance to Zenobia's former guard at the villa in Tibur, their rich, dark skin undeniably of African origin.

Still, Gaius had benevolently agreed to support her children until the age of five. It was an agreement she hoped she could amend when the time came. He displayed no rancor toward them, neither did he apply any fatherly affection for the twin children of the vanquished warrior queen. However, as their fifth birthdays approached, it became clear, he was in fact, a man who prided himself in keeping his word, right or wrong and could not be dissuaded from his original bargain. Either they would all three be banished into the countryside without any means of support, or Zenobia would carry on as his wife, and the children would be sent back to the country of their father's origin with sufficient funds to secure safe passage and a decent life.

Zenobia had no choice but endure her fate as she counted the days to their birthday when the conditions of their mutual agreement would be met out. Her heart was close to breaking, pressed relentlessly from both sides like the capstone of an arch. Once again, her treasure was being ripped away from her, never to be seen again. Sending them away was the only way her twins would gain any kind a stature in the world. Without the questor's continued support, all three of them would likely starve.

Zenobia had tried in vain to locate their father, Cyrus, a difficult task. The moment she had agreed to become Gaius's wife, Cyrus had been released from duty at the villa in Tibur and ordered to serve the Emperor in Britannia, in the far northern reaches of the Empire. Since then, she had been unable to learn anything of his existence, whether he had lived or died, or ever returned to Rome. It was her fervent wish that if there were any chance of reuniting the twins with their father, she could die at peace with the world.

With only three days until the deadline, a day that was bound to shatter her heart into unrecognizable pieces, a messenger arrived with startling news.

Cyrus had contacted Gaius through a trusted magistrate and was, after an exchange of a shipment of ivory from Auksum, appointed the twins' conservator, with the agreement he would have no contact with Zenobia.

She was beside herself with anxiety. Cyrus so close and no way to see him? It was a fate she could scarcely bear. But the thought of her children being delivered into the hands of their father gave her renewed hope for their future.

She returned to her chambers and uncovered the only trunk she had been allowed to carry with her from Palmyra. Inside was a cache of gold coins stamped with her image. Aurelian claimed the only way she could have won against the Roman army as long as she did was through magic and sorcery. And he was right. Zenobia's gift was a source of power, but not one taken lightly or used in the service of an unworthy cause. She had little need of it until now. She might never see her twins again, but she would not send them away empty handed.

"Send for the best goldsmith in the province," she ordered her woman servant. "Tell him he will be richly rewarded, but if he tells another soul, the warrior queen will see that he never uses his tongue to speak again."

"Yes, my lady," the servant said and hurried to carry out Zenobia's wishes.

*   *   *

Zenobia stood in the vestibule outside the goldsmith's workshop, heat waves shimmered over his kiln under a darkening sky. Thunder rumbled in the distance as her own mood darkened. There was a storm coming and she planned to take full advantage of its essence.

She moved in closer, heat warming her face as she watched embers build inside the clay dome. The goldsmith thrust metal tongs into the inferno and drew out a ceramic crucible. Zenobia moved in for a closer look. No sooner had he dropped another gold Zenobia coin into the crucible, than her image on its surface blurred, then spread, then disappeared into the growing, golden pillow at bottom of the vessel. Determination gathered in her chest, and right on cue, lightening flashed overhead, followed a few beats later by a rolling thunder that buoyed her spirit. Black clouds, hunched like a giant beast, rumbled closer at her unspoken command. She might be a prisoner in this world, but she still possessed the power that ruled her soul.

A dozen coins had gone into the crucible, soon to be poured into molds as described by Zenobia: Two identical serpent coils, designed to wrap around the upper arm of their owners.

"They seem a bit fearsome as bracelets go, for such sweet little children," the goldsmith commented. "Are you sure you wouldn't rather have something a little comelier? Matching pendants, perhaps with something more befitting. Hares, or birds? The viper seems a bit fearsome and pretentious."

Zenobia breathed deeply, considering carving out his tongue on the spot in punishment for his ignorance. But alas, if she maimed him, who would complete the casting of the coils and set the stones she'd removed from her own golden cuffs?

She let out an indulgent sigh. She may not respect his intellect, but she had to respect his craft. "There is a purpose to this, even though you may not see the value. We are talking about the children of the warrior queen, after all."

The goldsmith's eyes widened. It was suddenly obvious that whether he had forgotten who she was, or never known to begin with, he was in that moment enlightened. "How so? These are obviously too big for the young ones intended."

She was not in the habit of explaining herself to fools and she wasn't about to start now. Another flash of lightening lit their faces, followed by thunder closer still. Time was running out. She could not afford to waste any more of it.

She fixed her gaze on the man, all her royal presence focused on her intention. She was about to send her son and daughter out into the world, never to see them again. Whatever powers she had over men, whatever sorcerer spirit that had driven her to victory in the past, whatever love she still possessed for her offspring she would imbue into the gold.

Timeless, incorruptible, the gold was the medium and the serpent bracelets were the carrier that, charged with the might of the power that burned inside her, would bind them together for all eternity.

The goldsmith lifted his eyes to hers. "The gold is ready to pour into the molds."

Zenobia fixed him with the commanding glare of the warrior queen. He moved to prepare to pour from the crucible. "No!" She caught his forearm in a tight grip. "Not until I tell you. Are we clear?"

He nodded, swallowed hard, and held the crucible in the kiln's open maw, his grip white-knuckled on the heavy tongs.

Zenobia drew in a deep breath then lifted her eyes to the heavens and raised her arms over her head, hands spread in supplication.

"My beloved ones, wherever you travel in this world and the next, these golden vipers made from coins imbued with my power are your connection to me through eternity. With incorruptible gold I give you power, with these ruby eyes I give you the sight, and with the purity I give you love."

She closed her eyes and let the words gather in her mind, her heart, and her soul, then envisioned them flowing into the crucible, a swirling golden mist, gathering, assembling, then binding to the shining gold.

Lightning struck the metal tongs as thunder deafened her ears. The goldsmith's body jerked back, his arms blackened stumps.

"No!" she screamed. There was no more time. She grabbed the tongs away from him, pain searing through her uncovered hands. Gritting her teeth against the blistering pain, she walked the crucible to the molds and poured the liquid gold into the molds until they were full and she could no longer control her hands.

Exhausted, she slumped to the floor, the tongs slipped from her hands, the smell of burning flesh stinging her nostrils, pain erasing conscious thought.

When she came back to herself, the storm had retreated and a pathway to the heavens stretched across the sky. On the workbench where she had filled the molds, two perfectly cast bracelets coiled side by side, their ruby eyes gleaming in the half light.

How the rubies from her golden cuffs came to be embedded in their sockets was a mystery. The goldsmith lay dead more than ten feet away, but the twin bracelets, perfectly formed and coiled, lay finished on the slate bench. She cocked her head and watched transfixed as the serpents uncoiled, slid down the legs of the workbench, across the floor and slithered into her ruined hands, imparting a soothing coolness that took away all her pain.

She lifted her hands to eye level; the ruby eyes followed her gaze. She was bone weary and hollowed out, but as realization dawned, confidence once again filled the empty places in her heart. The coils, imbued with the power of her warrior's spirit and her mother's love, had fulfilled her intention. Indeed, they would be her enduring gift to her children. Her children, and their children, and theirs, and theirs, and theirs, would forever be bound together.

Healed and re-energized, she slipped the bracelets on her wrists and returned to her chambers.

The next morning, sitting on the edge of the fountain her husband had created for her, the bracelets glinted at her wrists as she ran her fingertips over the twin dolphin sculpture at the center, a perfectly matched pair carved in lapis stone. They were reminders he said, of the price she'd paid for their freedom.

"They're here, my lady."

Zenobia turned slowly at the sound of her woman servant's voice. That great hollow bubble that had been building in her breast since the day before began to deflate. After today, she would never see her children again, but because of the serpent's coils cast of her coins, she could send them out into the world knowing they would never be alone.

Zoey had changed her opinion of Victoria, aka *Kiki*, on the flight over from France. Hard to ignore a person when you're crammed into a center seat with the constant rumbling of the engines, the sounds and smells of three hundred cabin class passengers, and the prospect of never going home again looming in an unknown future.

Unlike the red-headed Fiona who'd been drool-snoring, her head against the tiny window almost since she'd taken her seat, Kiki white-knuckled a grip on the armrest the moment the giant airliner lifted its wheels off the runway. Zoe had come to enjoy that acceleration, her favorite part of the flight. She felt sorry for Kiki who obviously didn't share her delight during takeoff. Fighting the Gs pushing her into her seat, Zoey retrieved her bag from between her feet and found the box of *Raisinettes* Flora had bought her on the flight from Johannesburg.

She offered Kiki some of the chocolate covered raisins along with her friendliest smile. With a resigned sigh, Kiki let go of the armrest and held out a slender hand, allowing Zoey to drop a few into her palm.

As the plane leveled out, Kiki visibly relaxed. "It's not that great a privilege you know."

Zoey sent her a questioning brow. "What's not?"

"Dancing the lead." She cast her gaze into the aisle a moment as if to make sure Flora was still out of hearing distance up in first class.

It was true, Zoey could not take her eyes off the willowy blond when she danced. Her lines, her strength, her focus--no one in her class danced at her level. She would be hard to beat in a showdown. Now, she studied the girl's profile. Gone was the haughty facade, the disdainful glare, the challenge.

Kiki turned and the formerly cold light in her ice blue eyes warmed. "I see how you look at me at practice."

Zoey popped a handful of raisins in her mouth sucked the chocolate covering off. "What do you mean?"

Kiki looked away a moment as if she were sorry she'd brought up the subject. Then she turned back to Zoey and looked at her more directly with those glass blue eyes. "All I know is, the last girl who danced the lead -- Tabitha? The one whose place I took? -- They worked her *private shows.*"

"Private shows?"

"You know, one-on-one."

Zoey nodded slowly, but she wasn't exactly sure what she meant.

Kiki let go a low laugh, covered Zoey's hand on the armrest "How old are you?"

Apparently not old enough to understand her meaning exactly but remembering the look in her cousin's eye when he'd caught her alone, it didn't take much imagination to figure it out.

"Old enough," she murmured, munching another raisin.

Victoria pulled the flight magazine from the seat pouch in front of her and pretended interest in the pages, flipping one after another, too fast to read.

"After the regular performance" she confided, keeping her voice low, "some of the patrons ask for private performances. In London, after the final curtain, we were hustled back to our rooms for dinner and early to bed. But Tabitha didn't come back to the hotel until hours later. The rest of us shared a suite, but Flora gave Tabs a private room, probably so her late arrival wouldn't wake us, but I heard her come in."

Zoey shifted her bottom in the seat, not sure she wanted to hear all this, but Kiki went on.

"Tabitha and I got along pretty well, both from Cambridge and all. We usually talked about everything, you know? She was my best friend. So, when she didn't come in by midnight the night of our last performance, I waited up for her. Wanted to find out what she'd been doing. A party, maybe? Something fun and exciting I was missing out on. Maybe I'd work harder to knock her out of first position next time."

Well, that confirmed Zoey's suspicion. Victoria was a highly competitive dancer who would probably do anything--even topple a friend--if it meant dancing the lead on an international stage. It would be a shining gold star in any dancer's portfolio. One worth fighting for. "And so did you? Get to talk to her, I mean?"

Kiki rubbed her fingers into her temples hard. "I tried. I propped myself against our hotel room door so I could hear when she came in, but I fell asleep. It was three-thirty when the sounds next door finally woke me. I heard Tabi's voice, and a guy's. One of the stagehands, maybe? I couldn't tell. They were speaking in muffled voices. I waited until I heard him go back down the hall to the elevators, then I stuck my shoe in our door so it wouldn't lock me out and I knocked on Tabi's door."

Kiki turned toward Zoey then, leaning in close so their conversation could not be overheard. Her eyes narrowed with new intensity. "Zoey, you've got to promise me you won't tell another soul what I'm about to tell you."

Zoe refocused her attention. A chill gripped the nape of her neck, all the fears that first night in Paris sitting there on her shoulders, clamping down like raven's claws. So much drama. What did it have to do with her? She didn't want to hear what Kiki was about to say. Zoey wanted this dream of escape to continue. Wanted this path to be her way to a new life. But now, when she looked into Kiki's beautiful face, she saw her own doubts and disappointments reflected in those ice blue eyes. Victoria may be haughty and competitive but losing Tabitha had changed her. Victoria was still tough, and an incredibly talented dancer, but under all that she was frightened and alone. Zoey could identify with that. Zoey let out a breath she hadn't realized she was holding and gave Kiki a reluctant nod. "I promise."

Kiki took a long sip out of her water bottle then stuffed it back in the seat pocket. "When I knocked, at first Tabi didn't answer, so I got down low and whispered under the door. I knocked again and again, until finally, Tabi cracked open the door."

The look in Kiki's eyes conveyed her enduring fears. "She was holding a washcloth lumpy with ice to her cheek. Wouldn't let me in, wouldn't let me see, told me to go away.

"Oh my god! What did you do?"

"I told her I'd get Miss Flora to help, but Tabi grabbed my arm and cried, "No!" like telling would bring the devil down on our heads. Then she told me to go back to my room and don't tell anyone I'd seen her. Told me to mind my own business and everything would be all right. She wasn't all right though. She was scared. Really scared."

Zoey stared at her a long moment. There was a reason Tabi didn't want Kiki to tell Flora, and it couldn't be a good one.

"But that's not the worst of it." Kiki glanced down the aisle one more time, then leaned in again. "The next day, Tabs wasn't at breakfast. Neither was Miss Flora. Everyone else was asking what happened to her. I just kept my head down, like she said." She took Zoey's arm and squeezed tight, her eyes shining with unshed tears. "Zoe, I never *saw* her again. That's why I was so upset when we arrived in Paris. Flora didn't tell me until the morning of the flight I was taking Tabitha's place on the tour."

"You don't trust Flora?"

"She takes care of us. Buys our food, our clothes, everything. Without her, I might still be in a really bad situation back in London. But, after what happened to Tabi? I don't know."

Zoey studied her now. "But, if we can't trust Flora, who can we trust?"

Kiki slowly shook her head, then straightened. "*Shhh.* Here comes the cabin queen."

The flight attendant murmured her way down the aisle, offering snacks, gathering trash. "We're dimming the cabin lights for the next few hours girls, so please, keep your voices low. Passengers will be trying to get some sleep. This is the last snacks we'll be offering for a while."

Kiki snatched a handful of cookie packets and handed one to Zoe, dipping her head close again when the attendant was out of earshot. "That's the point, Zoe. Flora chose us for that reason. None of us has anyone, really. Does your family even know you're gone?"

"My..." The denial died on her lips. No, they didn't. The only person who knew she was gone was Shuda, and even she had no idea Roshana had changed her name. Unable to say the words out loud, she just shook her head.

Victoria unwrapped the cinnamon wafer and dunked it in the cooling cup of tea on her tray. "Way I see it, the only people we can trust right now are each other--you, me, Fiona."

"You're up early." Jamal's dad loaded the coffee grinder with fresh beans from his private stash and flipped the switch.

The aroma from fresh-ground coffee tingled Jamal's senses. He'd been up since three a.m. glued to his laptop to keep his mind from spinning about what he had to tell his father.

"Working my brochure," he said, which was mostly true. Since completing his home studies for the year, he'd turned all his attention on the reef restoration dive project his father had promised to fund if he could present him a good plan. All his attention, that is, until yesterday morning when he'd stepped across the threshold of Tessa's workshop.

He turned his laptop around so his dad could see the image on the screen. "Here's that great shot of me and the guys on the *Salacia* last summer. And, I scored these photos from the NOAA Coral Reef Conservation program." He zoomed in on the copy so his father could read the text. "I emailed their public relations department and the director said the photos are in the public domain, so I can use them."

His dad beamed him a smile, transferred the ground beans to the espresso machine he bought for Lexi's kitchen. "You've been busy."

"Yeah." Pressure built in Jamal's chest thinking about his inevitable confession. "I sort of copied your donation structure and the schedule highlights, California sites first, because of the extended diving season. I figure once we get those prospects signed up, we can make a wider distribution for later. The first broadcast email will go out to your regular donors."

Steaming up a generous dollop of milk foam, his father sat down next to him. "So you hacked my mailing list? And when did you plan on sharing that information with me?"

Jamal gave him a sheepish grin. "I just did." His nerves spread tenterhook tight.

"Sounds like a good plan to me," his father returned.

Jamal cleared his throat. "Yeah. And I'm... building an interest list on *Instagram*. Any kid fifteen and up following reef diving with the means to join our first expedition will get the link to the brochure. Plus, I've got a batch being printed to hand out at yacht clubs from here to San Diego. Not everybody's parents are on *Insta*. We could start seeing responses tomorrow."

His father sent him an appraising look that spread into a wide smile. "I'm proud of you, son. It's one thing to have a dream, but quite something different to actually sit down and do the work to make it happen."

True that. In more ways than one. Jamal pressed his lips together, feeling his cheeks burn. There was just that one little snag in his plan. He blinked at the screen, his fingers poised on the keys. He closed his eyes and let himself feel her again, that warm presence spooned against his back, their heartbeats coming into sync, her need feeding into his strength, the terrible, gut-wrenching separation.

Tessa had given him twenty-four hours to tell his father about the incident in her workshop before she blew his secret right out of the water.

Now, with the prospect looming before him and only a couple of hours left to keep his promise, the idea of telling his father what he'd done felt like looking up from a deep free dive afraid you didn't have enough air to make it to the surface.

Coffee in hand, his dad was headed toward the kitchen door.

He's getting away. Do it. Now. He took a deep breath and stood. "Dad? There's, ah, something else."

Zaire turned in the doorway licking foam off his upper lip. "Hum?"

How to start. Ugh. Maybe it would have been better to let Tessa tell his father after all. But, no. If he was going to help his sister he'd have to do this himself.

The fact that he had a sister out there somewhere had been news to all of them and was still a topic they were having trouble finding words to discuss. But there was nothing else for it. He was convinced she needed him and that meant he had to take a risk.

The cleft between his father's eyes deepened. He sat in front of him. "What's up, son? You look worried. Was everything all right with your finals? Because we can always--"

"No. It's not that." Worried? He wasn't worried. He was terrified. Not just that he could lose the trust he had worked so hard to build with Zaire, his dad, but that everything he'd witnessed the day before might have already happened and he was too late to do anything about it.

He jammed his fingers into his hair and raked them through. Every dive starts with a long, deep breath, right? He bit his bottom lip and took it. "I went into Tessa's workshop. Saw something." The confession came out of his mouth on a wave of nausea.

He swallowed it down as he watched emotions play across his father's face. Confusion, disappointment, concern. But the fear, the nausea faded the moment his father returned to the table and sat down. "All right. Tell me."

He listened intently while Jamal told him everything that had happened since Rags grabbed his shoe and ran into Tessa's workshop; how the golden serpent's coil bracelet slithered up his arm, the blood on the bunk of the luxury berth on a vessel he didn't recognize, the sense his sister had possibly been on the scene of a horrific crime. Then to seal the deal, he lifted his shirt sleeve and showed his father the red mark the gold bracelet had branded his biceps.

Zaire raked fingers through his hair, drew in a long breath, then leaned in, resting his elbows on the table. Jamal held his breath. This was it. He was going to be grounded for life. To his relief, his father wanted confirmation. "And you say you felt your sister in that space?"

Jamal licked his lips, nodded. "I think she's in trouble, Dad. Bad trouble."

"What did Tessa have to say about it?"

Jamal pushed out his breath. Oh my gosh. Oh. My. Gosh. "Uh, she… wants to do a session. Says I might get more detail so we can—"

"No." Zaire pushed away from the table. "You're not putting that bracelet on again."

"But Zaire—Dad… "

"Let Lex or Tessa do it. They have the experience, the history."

"But I have the *connection*, Dad. And what I saw was in the now, not in the past. That girl? The one I saw being carried out of the fancy cabin? She might have been dead. And I could feel my sister's presence in that same room. She had to have been there in that cabin at one point. If she witnessed what happened? She could be in danger, too."

There was movement at the doorway. They both turned to see Lexi standing in her terry robe, her hair wrapped up in a towel, toothbrush poised at her mouth.

Her gaze shifted between them in silence for a beat, then slowly lowered her brush. "What?"

His dad motioned for her to sit down. "You need to hear this."

Jamal blinked at his mom and dad across the table. It was still a new experience, the three of them united after years apart.

Lexi unwrapped the towel and ran her fingers through her curls, sending his father some serious shade. "Face it, Zai. Tess and I used the jewelry to travel and we're both here to tell about it. If Jam's got a lead on his sister, I don't see how we can refuse."

His father paced the room. "I'm just afraid--"

"I'm not," Jamal blurted. That wasn't actually true. He was scared shitless. But he couldn't let that stop him.

Lexi's phone vibrated on the table, grabbing all their attention. She glanced at it then got up, shooting them a weak smile.

"Hey, Tess," she answered, putting her on speaker phone.

"You dressed?"

"No, but getting there, what's up?"

"Um... There's someone here to see you."

"Someone to see me? At your house?"

"It was the last address she had for you. It's urgent, she says."

Lexi looked confused, which was weird because Lexi always had her act together, which was why Jamal liked her from the start. Why he trusted her.

She glanced at his dad. "A client maybe? I don't know."

Zaire shook his head. "Better go. But hurry back. Jamal and I have something urgent to discuss with you, too."

"So," Lexi said in the phone, hesitating long enough to give Jamal a funny feeling in his gut. "Tell her I'll be right there." She wrapped her robe around her and hurried next door.

Lexi stopped at the back door to Tessa's kitchen, disbelief knotted in her throat. No. It couldn't be. The woman stood at the balcony facing the grand canal, hands clamped tight around the railing.

At the sound of the door closing, the woman turned just slightly. Recognition hit Lexi like a sharp fist to the sternum. Though it had been nearly fifteen years, she knew that posture, those near knotty shoulders, that unmistakable profile.

"Mother."

Althea Tedese-Hill turned fully around, her expression stony. She looked Lexi up and down, and then the familiar judgmental pinch crimped the corners of her mouth. "I suppose I should have gone to the hotel first and given you time to dress."

Lexi pulled her robe tighter around her and cinched the tie belt. "I… thought you were a client."

Althea's brow went up. "That's interesting. You meet clients in your bathrobe?"

Lexi returned her rude scrutiny. Surprised to see her mother was dressed in traditional Kente cloth, something she had forbidden Lexi to ever do. But she wasn't surprised that after fifteen years the first words out of her mother's mouth were cutting and cold.

Lexi fought the urge to turn and stomp down the stairs. She bit down her angry response and asked the obvious question. "What on earth are you doing here?"

Althea lifted that sharp chin and huffed out a heavy breath. "I'm... afraid I have some... disturbing news."

Lexi stared at her mother, speechless.

Tessa nudged Lexi from behind, and whispered, "Want me to get Zaire?"

"No," Lexi said reaching behind her to grab her friend's hand for support. She bit her lip. "Just... you stay."

She fixed her eyes on her mother, wondering what could possibly be more disturbing than seeing her standing in Tessa's kitchen. She crossed her arms over her chest, willing her heartbeat to settle. "Go on."

"It's about your daughter," her mother blurted, then stalked out of the kitchen into Tessa's living room and dropped heavily onto the leather sofa there.

Lexi followed her, feeling the dam of fifteen years of silence starting to crack. It took her another moment and a deep breath to find her words, and when they came to the surface, she didn't have the will to hold anything back.

"All these years, nothing. Then you show up with news about my daughter as if you'd known about her all along?" Voicing a long standing hurt left her hollow and empty.

"It's… a long story. But I beg you, please. Just listen."

Her mother, begging? Now that was a surprise. She took a moment to actually look at the woman sitting before her. Under the stark exterior and bright yellow Kente cloth, she looked travel worn and gaunt. Her mother's judgment came out stern and stoic, but she looked frail, emaciated. Her life had obviously not been a picnic since leaving her father. Or maybe it was something more present, like ill health. Some of Lexi's pent-up anger and resentment melted away. If Lexi didn't reserve her own judgment, she would be just like her mother.

She relaxed her shoulders, slid her hands into the big, warm pockets of her robe.

"Can I get you something to drink? Coffee? Juice?"

Her mother let her head fall back against the seat cushion, let out a breath that seem to deflate her. "Some juice would be wonderful. Thank you."

Lexi stood alone at the kitchen counter a moment, gathering her thoughts. She wasn't a child anymore, subject to her mother's constant disapproval. But she'd learned a lot in her profession. Things were not always as they seemed. Sometimes it was more helpful to be silent and listen. Show some compassion. Her mother looked awful, after all. Not anything like the elegant professor who dropped her off at a private school all those years ago and never came back.

She poured herself a glass of juice as well, if for no other reason than to have something to hold on to, then went back to the living room, and passed a juice to her mother.

Althea closed her eyes a moment, nodded slowly. "I know this isn't fair, Alexis. You have no reason to do anything but throw me out of here." She sipped tentatively from the glass. "I haven't been the best mother--"

Lexi reached down deep inside her for that compassion, but it simply was not there. All the anger she'd pushed down over the years boiled over like a forgotten pan on the stove. "Haven't been the best? Are you kidding me? You lie to me about having twins, stick me in a school all the way across the country from you and I never hear from you again? I had to read about my father's passing in a *Politico* article, for god's sake. And now you have disturbing news? What? What could be more disturbing? Huh? Because all that's pretty goddamned disturbing, don't you think?"

Her mother sat up and placed the glass carefully on the coffee table, then folded her hands in her lap and raised her eyes to Lexi's. "Your daughter was living with my sister in Gaborone."

"Your sister!"

Tessa squeezed her hand, leaned into her ear and said low, "Just listen. Hear her out."

Lexi grit her teeth against the sudden urge to gag. Her daughter has lived with her Aunt in Botswana all these years? Not a word? Years of self-blame and worry gathered in her stomach. She had clung to the dream that her daughter had been placed with a good family and was living a happy life. If she had known the truth, she would have gone after her years ago. Reclaimed her right as her mother. White hot anger drove up her throat and threatened to choke her. Tessa tightened her grip on her arm.

"My sister called me a week ago," her mother went on, anguish clear in her voice. "Roshana didn't come home from dance practice. They checked with her best friend and she wasn't there. They reported her missing to the authorities. She's simply disappeared. We've searched everywhere. I thought maybe she had found you on her own and managed somehow to come here."

Dance practice? Best friend? Her name was Roshana?

Lexi couldn't breathe. Her mother's lips were moving, but all she heard was the name repeating inside her head: *Roshana, Roshana, Roshana.* All she remembered of her daughter was her precious weight in her arms, a tiny cry, a fist flailing up at a cruel world from under a pink blanket. And the name she'd secretly given her. Ruby.

Tessa pulled her close. "Lex? Honey? It's okay. You're okay. Breathe."

Lexi drew in a long, slow breath. Yes. She was okay. Barely.

She swallowed down her anger, her disgust, her guilt. There would be time for that later. This wasn't news after all. Jamal had already seen it. He'd told her weeks ago. His sister was in trouble. And what had she done? Nothing.

Who cared what led up to the situation. They had to act. Now.

Her mother stood, started to reach out. "Alexis, listen. I'm not asking you to forgive me. I'm asking for your help."

Lexi stood, wrapping her arms around her middle, searching her mother's face. There was no pinched judgment, no accusation, no posturing. Just the fact of her daughter's existence hanging in the air between them like a ragged cloud. Considering all her mother had hidden, all she had destroyed, and who she was, it must have taken a mountain of humility and courage to get on a plane and fly all the way around the world to admit what she had done.

"I know you're angry," Althea said, looking away. Her voice low and full of pain. "You have good reason to be. But please know this. I always wanted to tell you. I just... I mean..." Her eyes lifted to

Lexi's. "I was a coward, Alexis. Selfish and vain. I don't deserve forgiveness. But… Roshana is out there, I tell you. She needs our help."

Lexi unwrapped her arms and let out a heavy sigh. As much as she wanted to order her mother out of Tessa's house, as much as she wanted to punish her for all she had done and all she had not, she could not deny the fact that something had brought them together. The fact that Jamal had felt his sister's presence and her mother had turned up on her doorstep with the same feeling could not be a coincidence. Now was definitely not the time to get bound up in old hurts and battles. They had much more urgent work to do. She lifted her gaze to Tessa, then fixed her eyes on her mother. "We need to go next door."

Jamal watched Phillip pace the room until he stopped suddenly, his *private investigator* hat firmly in place. He fixed his gaze on Jamal. "What can you tell us about the cabin?"

Jamal frowned, rubbed absently at the raw skin on his arm. He'd been so freaked at the sight of the blood in his vision, the girl's hair spilling over the floor as she was carried from the room, he hadn't really focused on the surroundings. Now he closed his eyes, forcing himself to remember the images he'd seen, but nothing came.

Frustrated, he rubbed the gold coin and tried again. As it warmed in his fingers, the scene began to appear in his memory. He relaxed and described what he saw. "The yacht was new. Fancy. Not the biggest stateroom I've seen, but bigger than dad's stateroom on the *Salacia*."

"Fancy. Like a cruise ship?" his father asked.

Jamal fixed his gaze on his him a moment then shook his head. "No. Not commercial like that. Rich dude fancy, like some of your donors at Fifth Street Landing."

Zaire's brows shot up.

Phillip scooted himself into the table. "Fifth Street Landing?" He typed purposefully on his laptop keyboard.

His father pushed his cup away. "I've done a few fund raisers there. It's a luxury mooring in San Diego harbor. Three-hundred-foot, transpacific grade. Some corporate owned, some private, some charters. All of them disgustingly over the top in every possible way."

Phillip drew in a breath and held it a moment before he let it out, scrunching up his nose. "Epstein disgusting?"

His father frowned, leaned against the kitchen counter. "Not out of the question," he said low.

The idea of his sister involved in something so sinister hit Jamal hard in the gut.

His fear must have showed on his face because Phillip sent him a sympathetic look. "With the teenage girls involved, we can't ignore the fact that there's a robust human trafficking trade right here in California. San Diego is a notoriously strong port of entry. Private vessels do have to deal with customs coming into the country, but if the vessel was registered in the Port of San Diego they wouldn't have to register."

Jamal felt sick.

Phillip went on. "The good news is, if what you saw was right, we could have chance to track one down." He swiveled his laptop so Jamal and his dad could see. It was a luxury yacht rental site offering party boats at the level Jamal had described. He scrolled a moment, then clicked. "Check this one out."

Jamal stared at the screen. It was like _Zillo_ for boats. Ships, really, by the descriptions. He scrolled through the photos, dining decks, pools, galleries, staterooms... His vision could have been any one of them. A chill spiked up his spine.

He shifted his gaze to his father. "Feels right, but I get nothing specific. Crap. This could take days."

Phillip pined his father with a serious gaze. "If he uses the coin and the bracelet in a controlled environment--"

The kitchen door opened. All three of them looked up. Lexi and Tessa came in, followed by a tall, black woman in a bright Kente cloth skirt and silky yellow shirt. Recognition jolted Jamal to his feet. It was the woman who had started him on this journey. His lips went cold. What was she doing here?

Zaire stood, mouth agape. "Mrs. Hill?" He scooted a chair away from the table and offered it to her.

The woman ignored his father, her gaze fixed on Jamal, boring through him like she was some kind of supernatural priestess. Or at least, that's where his imagination took him. That day in Bole, she'd showed up out of nowhere and dropped a bomb on him that completely changed his life and his father's, too. His hand went unconsciously to the coin at his neck laying warm against his skin. "What are you doing here?"

Her eyes roamed over his face, taking in every feature like seeing him for the first time, then she lifted her chin, pinned her gaze on him like she'd been reading his mind. "I think you already know."

*　　　*　　　*

Lexi's stomach took a dip. Having her mother in the room pushed all the buttons she'd managed to hide. Anger, abandonment, rejection. Now her mother, the one who had lied to her for fifteen years was suddenly back, asking for help, looking needy and frail, making crazy assertions. How was she supposed to react to that?

And then, like he sensed her discomfort, her pain, Zaire's arms came around her from behind, and his smooth baritone voice vibrated against her back. "Jamal, why don't you fill your mother in on what we've been doing while she was next door?"

Jamal ignored Zaire's request, and to Lexi's surprise, he focused on Althea. "I want to know why you did what *you* did."

Startled, mouth agape, Althea stared at Jamal a long moment, and then as if she'd lost the strength to stand, she dropped herself into the chair Zaire had offered.

"What do you mean, young man?"

Lexi couldn't help feeling a little proud of her son. He was young, but ever since they'd learned the truth about each other, he never missed a chance to say what was on his mind.

"You broke our family," he said, matter-of-factly, letting that statement hang in the air between them a moment before he went on. "I would have understood putting us up for adoption. My parents were too young to make a family. But you lied and you could have fixed it, but you didn't. It hurt my mom. Hurt all of us. And my sister? She's out there all alone now and doesn't even know we care, and that's on you."

Lexi reached out and put her hand gently on his wrist, a familiar ache building at the back of her throat. Her son was standing up for her, Zaire's warmth supported her. Her mother would have reminded him to respect his elders. But Lexi wasn't her mother, thank god. Jamal had a right to answers. They all did.

Althea wrung her hands under Jamal's steady gaze. "I… did what I thought was right at the time." Her voice, a low whisper, cracked a little before she shifted her gaze to Lexi. "I had my career to protect, my reputation."

Oh, boy hadn't she heard that before.

Then focusing on Jamal, Althea went on, "I had the sight, like you, all the time I was growing up. My family were all Christians, but they respected the old ways. In Addis Ababa having a connection to ancestors was considered a magical gift. Respected. But in the academic world?" She huffed out a laugh. "Not so much. Once I met your grandfather, I pushed my gift down deep. No one in Washington DC wants to listen to some fool spout about connection spells and seeing into the past or the future."

To Lexi, she went on, "You can hide it, even from yourself, but it doesn't go away. That day I realized you were pregnant, I *saw* that you were having twins. I'd *seen* it all before, in my visions. There would be twins and they would complete an ancient spell. I didn't want to believe any of it. I was supposed to be this down-to-earth professor at the university, married to a diplomat, for God's sake, not some crazy charlatan with visions of the past, of... magic spells. I had to protect myself, protect my reputation. What would people think?" She sank deep into her bones and seemed to lose her momentum a moment. Then she started again, her voice low, almost a keen. "I was wrong. I know that now. I was protecting the wrong things. Loved the wrong things."

A tear streaked down her cheek. Lexi blinked at her a moment. *Unbelievable.* She passed her a napkin. Silence sat heavy in the kitchen, while Althea dabbed at her eyes. "When I got sick, the visions became more intense—wouldn't leave me be. Accused me. Haunted me." She looked up at Lexi. "My time was running out. That's when I went to see Jamal, in Bole, told him about you. But before I could manage to leave Ethiopia for my sister's in Gaborone, tell Roshana what I'd done, I got worse." She blotted her eyes again, let out a tired sigh.

Lexi slipped out of Zaire's arms, pulled out a chair and sat down next to her mother. "Got worse?" she prompted, her voice soft and full of the concern. There would be a time for retribution, but that time wasn't now.

Althea looked out over the Grand Canal where the tide was going out. She rolled her lips in a moment before she went on. "I have breast cancer. Stage four. There's... nothing more can be done. Not the inheritable kind, thank the gods, but... "

She watched a pair of gulls land on the little dock out front, their squawking the only sounds in the air as she seemed to gather her strength. "After I talked to Jamal back in Bole, I went into a care facility in Addis Ababa, did some chemo, worked through a recovery period." She shrugged her shoulders, shook her head, then went on, "By the time I was strong enough to travel and got to my sister's in Gaborone, Roshana was gone."

Lexi sat back in her chair, disbelief settling in her soul.

*   *   *

Jamal felt a pang of regret for putting the old woman through all that, but he was glad he had. His mother needed to hear it, and it fortified his own story in a way. "Well... I know where she is. At

least," he said, hesitating, glancing at his father, "…
we think we can find her." He sat down and felt the
tension in the room dial back a notch. "Phillip found
a website that shows party boats for rent."

"And you think your sister might be on one of
them?" Althea asked.

"It feels right," Jamal said. "It's a place to start."

"It's a long shot," Phillip said. "If those vessels
are TransPac cruisers, they could be anywhere in the
world. Althea says your sister left Gaborone only a
few days ago."

"He's right," his father said. "What makes you
think she's on one near here all of a sudden?"

"Proximity," Jamal insisted. "Just like when you
can see some of our close neighbors' Wi-Fi
connections on our computer, but not ones a few
blocks over. What I mean is, I think I'm feeling her
now because she's close. Closer than she's ever been.
And, she could have flown around the world in two
days on a jumbo jet."

Althea looked up then. "He's got the vision,
Alexis. Like I said. They both have."

Lexi stared at Jamal. "Is that true son?"

Jamal licked his lips, sending her a sheepish look.
"I… never thought of it as some kind of vision, but,
you know, I've been wearing the necklace all my life.
I sensed a presence from it. I never could figure out
what that meant, until dad and I came here. That

was the first time I knew it was... It was *her*. And then, when I was in Tessa's workshop... "

He grabbed a cookie and twisted it apart, then focused on Lexi again. "She feels me, too. And, dad and I have been planning our reef project to depart from San Diego Harbor. The yachts Phillip just showed me are in San Diego Harbor. It can't be a coincidence."

Lexi leveled her gaze on him a long time. He hoped that was a good thing. After a moment, the skepticism he saw on her face faded under that familiar Lexi smile. "So... man with the vision," she said, lifting a brow. "What's our next move?"

Jamal blinked at her a moment, before his face lit up with understanding. "I want Tessa to hypnotize me. It worked for you guys." He looked at his dad, expectantly. "I trust Tessa, dad. So does mom."

Zaire rubbed his fingers over his mouth and paced the room a moment, then turned to face the group. "I was skeptical before Althea showed up. But it looks like all the forces are coming together." He shifted his gaze to Lexi. "We'd be foolish at this point not to give it a try. I say we let him do it. If she's on one of those party boats... " The worry returned to his eyes.

Jamal jumped up, pumped a fist in the air. "Yes!"

Jet engines droned on and on in Zoey's head. Would this flight never end? The first-class flight from Johannesburg to Paris had been easy, with earplugs and blankets and eye pillows and a never-ending supply of tea, and sweet and salty snacks. Travel in the main cabin was a rude awakening. It was Zoey's first glimpse of the truth that all was not a bed of roses in the Florabunda dance company.

Tall for her age, her knees nearly touched the seat in front of her. Stuck between Kiki on one side and Fiona on the other, both of them using her shoulders for a pillow, she could scarcely move, let alone stretch out. At four hours into the flight, exhaustion gave way to droning white noise, and she finally drifted off into a twilight sleep. Under its spell, her thoughts caromed between wild fantasies of dancing before rapt crowds and a longing for the young man she had only seen in her dreams yet seemed to know her right down to her bones. Then, like a candle in the dark, he appeared in her mind, the tall boy she had seen in her dreams slipped his hand in hers.

She wasn't alone after all.

Startled awake by a passenger making his way down the narrow aisle toward the restroom, Zoey gripped the necklace at her throat and scrunched her eyes closed tight, longing to hold on to that face, that presence, that anchor in her life, but it was no use. The lights came up in the cabin, bringing Zoey fully awake.

Kiki lifted her head off Zoey's shoulder, drowsy eyed. "Are we landing?"

Zoey clicked the video on the console to look at the map with the airplane progressing across the screen. "We're pretty close."

"Have you seen Flora?"

"No. Not since she collected our papers." She had come through the cabin, speaking to each of the girls, reminding them what to say when they passed through customs, collecting their papers so she could photograph each and every one. They were traveling in a dance company under her supervision and she was responsible.

Kiki sat up and stretched, flipped her ponytail from behind her back to drape over her shoulder, then leaned into to Zoey's ear and spoke, keeping her voice low. "So you agree, you keep all that I've told you to yourself?"

"Absolutely," Zoey said. "I don't want to upset Fiona more than we have to." Kiki leaned forward and smiled at the younger girl. "At least until we get into the States."

Zoey let out her breath. "So, what are you going to do?"

"Flora told me there would be some special training for me as the lead, and that hasn't happened yet. I think I need to play along, because if I don't--"

Fiona lifted her head and yawned. "Don't what?" she asked sleepily.

"Oh, hey, sleepy head," Zoey said. She didn't want to think about the *because*. And Kiki was right about getting into the United States. Without Flora and the dance company cover, they would probably send her straight back to Bots and her aunt's not-so-caring protection. She rolled her shoulder, restoring the circulation. "If I don't go to the ladies room soon, I'm going to pee my pants."

Fiona giggled, gathered her hair into a Scrunchie. "Me too."

Kiki unfastened her seatbelt and stood in the aisle. "Let's all go before everybody in this frickin' cabin wakes up. If we're going to land soon, they'll want us back in our seats."

Zoey's thoughts played ping pong in her head as they made their way through the cabin. She'd seen all the girls dance and it was pretty clear. Before this Tabitha lost her place as the lead, Zoey could easily have been third in line for the lead position, just behind Kiki. With Tabitha gone, now Zoey was likely second. She was that much closer to having her dream. But, now that she and Victoria were friends, it was harder to see herself in a battle with her for first place. Still, you never knew when your competitor might make a mistake or fall and take herself out. She didn't want to think about that because she didn't want something to happen to Kiki. Not if it meant she disappeared.

When they returned to their seats, Flora was making her way down the aisle. She handed them back their paperwork. "Now listen carefully," she said, the corners of her eyes crinkled with fatigue. "When we get off the plane, I want you to stay at the gate until I do a head count. Just move off to the right and stay by the windows. We'll be going through customs as a group, do you understand?"

The three of them looked at each other and nodded their heads. Zoey was still trying to come to grips with the idea they were actually landing in the United States.

"Okay. We'll be taking a helicopter to the ship from there."

"Helicopter?" Kiki squeaked.

Fiona's eyes rounded. "Ship?"

"Wow. How will we all fit in a helicopter?" Zoey asked, excitement at the prospect of riding in a helicopter bubbled in her chest, masking her earlier fears.

"Four at a time. I'll go with the first group and Chantal will wait till the last."

"But a helicopter? I'm not sure I can..." Fiona fidgeted, looked down the aisle as if she had a choice in the matter. "I thought we were dancing in San Diego."

Flora smiled at the youngest in the company and shook her head. "The *Josephine* is like a cruise ship, Fi. Like I said, you'll be dancing for some of the most notable people in the world." She glanced at Victoria. "Some of you will have private rooms."

Kiki looked away, laced her fingers together, and gripped her hands tight in her lap.

Zoey's heart did a little flip. *Josephine.* The name sent her images of a tall black dancer wearing nothing but a skirt made of bananas. Josephine Baker had been a superstar; her dancing considered scandalous in America. But in Europe she was an idol. Zoey imagined herself flipping her hips in a banana skirt.

"Hold on to your papers," Flora reminded them, bringing her back to reality. Her expression was stern again. "They're the only thing keeping you from going back where you came from."

*　　　*　　　*

Zoey, Fiona, Kiki, and Flora were on the first flight to the *Josephine* from the airport. An overwhelming rush of excitement in Zoey's chest gave way to a queasy surge when the chopper lifted off the tarmac and lurched forward at a steep angle. Fiona dug her fingers into Zoey's arm. A moment later they were whomp, whomp, whomping their way over the water of the bay where massive aircraft carriers and cruise ships that looked like floating hotels dwarfed small pleasure craft and commercial fishing boats. A line of cars crossed a soaring bridge.

The helicopter pilot's voice crackled through their headphones. "That's Coronado Island over there, and in a minute you'll see the USS Midway museum."

Zoey gripped her necklace like a life preserver and pressed her cheek against the window to try to see out while engine vibrations rattled her bones. Her chest nearly burst with longing. She knew nothing about California's West Coast. Her grandmother had only mentioned Washington DC as her birthplace. But this place called to her like the constant pull she felt whenever she saw that familiar face in her dreams, a pull that had gotten stronger and stronger until, when she finally saw the Pacific Ocean stretching out before her, she knew without question, she was in the right place.

This trip had nothing to do with running away from her cousin's relentless jeering, or dancing her way into a new life, or getting to fly first class and then on a helicopter. This trip, this fantasy fulfilled, had everything to do with coming closer to the boy in her dreams. Without that pull toward him, she would never have tried to leave.

With a sudden pitch that shoved her away from the window against Fiona, they began a circling descent and headed toward a massive yacht that dwarfed every other boat in the marina below.

"Oh my god, it has its own swimming pool," Fiona squealed, clapping her hands. "This is going to be amazing."

Zoey's stomach clenched as the pilot hovered the craft over the heliport on the bow and lowered them noisily to the deck. No sooner had they climbed out of the chopper and hurried across the deck to a windowed reception area than the helicopter lifted off again and angled back toward San Diego International Airport.

Fiona and Zoey hurried to follow Kiki as she strode toward the reception area, her head held high like she boarded a luxury yacht every day of her life. All eyes were on her, as usual. But as Zoey moved in next to Kiki at the counter, she couldn't shake the feeling at least one person's eyes were on her. Bending to surreptitiously adjust the handle on her carry-on bag, she turned her head slightly to see that indeed, a dark-haired man in casual, sand-colored pants and a white dress shirt with no tie was giving her an appraising look. He sat in a club chair near the reception desk like he was waiting to meet someone.

Now he looked at her with eyes so pale she wondered for a moment if there might be something wrong with them. He gave her a slight smile as though he was used to people staring. His shirt lay open at the neck to display a heavy gold chain with a gaudy medallion weighing it down. He was good looking for an older guy. Took good care of himself.

A couple of women who looked like they'd just stepped into the lobby from the pool stood behind him, one whispered in his ear, pointing at Kiki. Zoey looked away as the girls made their way to the reception desk where a porter waited to load their bags on a cart.

Zoey crunched stray hair into her top knot and pulled her skirt down into place as a petite brunette in a metallic gold tank dress that left nothing to the imagination called to Flora from an arched doorway. "Hello, hello! Welcome aboard!"

They embraced like long lost pals, air kissing each other's cheeks before *metallic woman* turned to the girls. "I'm Angelica, and I'll be coordinating everything for you ladies while you're here. If you have any problems, don't call the porters, let Flora know and I'll take care of all your needs. The rooms are ready. I can't wait to see you all at the dress rehearsal," she crooned, excitedly, her eyes beaming. "Which one of you is Victoria?" She stretched out the name to add to the drama.

She clasped bejeweled hands together, her moves exaggerated like she was putting on a performance. She scanned their faces expectantly, her gaze landing on Kiki.

Of course it did. Without saying a word, Victoria commanded attention with her long, wheat blond hair; tall, willowy profile, and electric blue eyes. She raised her hand, unnecessarily. "It's Kiki, but yeah."

Angelica sorted through a handful of room key cards and handed one to Kiki. "Okay, so you have your own suite," she said, handing Fiona and Zoe their own cards, "And you two will share the suite across the hall."

Kiki exchanged glances with Zoey. Zoey's stomach took a little dip. They had agreed not to split up.

"I thought we would all share, you know, like before?" Kiki's eyes plead her case to Flora. Zoey doubted it would make any difference, and she was right.

"Oh no, love," Flora crooned, confirming her fears. "You're the lead now. You get your own suite. The girls will be right across the hall. You'll love it. I promise."

She spread her arms and herded them out of the reception area into Angelica's care. "Now find your rooms and get yourselves cleaned up. I want us to run through a dress rehearsal before tonight's show."

Zoey's heart slammed into her throat. "Show? Tonight?" Her voice sounded more desperate than she intended, but she couldn't help herself. It was exciting, but it was all happening too fast, like an accident in progress, each step leading closer to a massive collision and there was nothing she could do to stop it.

The porter scooted out the door into the hallway with their cart.

"Well, of course, tonight," Angelica said in a honeyed voice. "We'll set sail as soon as the rest of your company boards and head out into international waters. The main performance--that's *you*--starts at 10:00 p.m."

Flora fixed them with her mother-hen look. "Chantal will bring all your costumes to your rooms in..." she paused a second and checked her phone. "Two hours. Now, go with Angelica."

Kiki and Fiona stared at her, their mouths comically open, and Zoey joined them.

"Well, chop, chop," Flora said, clapping her hands. Her eyes flashed to the man sitting in the club chair a moment before she explained, "I'm staying here until the rest of the girls arrive."

Zoey couldn't help but smile when Fiona hurled herself onto a full-sized sofa covered in sea-blue velvet. A console table behind the sofa held a sculpture of twin dolphins thrusting out of a wave, the ultimate image of freedom.

Zoey stalked the space, her heartbeat climbing up her throat, her prescient senses shifting into overdrive in a way she had not experienced before. She was nervous. That was for sure. She'd never been on a boat before. From the moment she set foot on the deck, alarm bells started going off in her head. She'd convinced herself there was nothing to be afraid of. But here, in this stateroom, the noise in her head amplified, then sharpened to a high-pitched scream. Glancing around the room, no one else seemed aware of the warning, but her heartbeat refused to settle. Her fingers sought her necklace, then clasped the coin, her anchor. *Whatever it is, we can deal, right?*

She opened her eyes to find herself standing behind the dolphin sculpture, their polished lapis-lazuli skin glowing under overhead lights trained directly on it. She let go of the necklace, drawn to the sculpture. The moment her hands rested on each of the dolphin's backs, the screaming in her head stopped and her heartbeat settled.

Angelica's voice pierced the calm. "Be careful of the art pieces in here, girls. The owner's a collector. These pieces are..."

"Ancient," Zoey whispered, then pulled in a long, slow breath. She'd dreamed about dolphins only last night. Twin dolphins circled and leapt at the bow of a boat as it cut through the water...

Angelica turned her away from the artwork. "Right, so no touching."

Another delighted *squee* grabbed Zoey's attention. There was a wet bar and a fridge with every kind of liquor one could imagine showing through the glass door. There was a tray of cheeses, grapes, and crackers on a highly polished wood counter that separated the living area from a small kitchenette. A set of sliding doors opened onto a covered balcony with a jetted tub tucked into a private corner.

Zoe stepped into the bedroom where there were two double-sized beds loaded with pillows and framed in the same polished wood as the kitchen. They were side by side with matching chests of drawers along the inside wall. At the far end was a bathroom fit for a queen, wall-to-wall mirrors, a shower and sunken tub, a massage table, and another wet bar. Another set of sliding glass doors opened onto the same veranda as the main room.

Kiki slipped her hand into Zoey's. "I guess we could share one of those bunks," she said softly into her ear.

"Yours is across the hall," Angelica said to her with a cordial smile.

"Sure," Kiki said. "I got that." Her eyes slid back to Zoe.

"Yeah. We're good," Zoe added. "She can find it." She led the way back to the main part of the cabin toward the door and stood beside it until Angelica wafted out.

"See you in two hours," she said, "And remember, these doors lock automatically, so don't forget your keys when you go out."

Kiki sank onto the sofa, her face glum. "How long did Flora say we'd be here?"

Fiona tried to open the liquor cabinet in the fridge with no luck. "Three shows, I think. At least I thought I remembered Flora saying something about a dry first night, then two more shows."

Dry first night? What did that mean? On a ship named *Josephine*, after what Kiki had told her, Zoey was afraid to speculate.

"Well. We've got two hours till dress rehearsal. Who wants the bathroom first?"

CHAPTER 12 – THE POINT OF NO RETURN

Engines thrummed to life somewhere in the bowels of the vessel and gradually grew stronger, sending an anxious vibration through Zoey's body as she stepped out of the shower. Chantal had brought their costumes to the suite and left them laid out on their beds.

By the time they were dressed for rehearsal, a quick look out the sliding doors confirmed they were heading out of the harbor toward open ocean. Zoey took a moment to stand at the balcony while they waited for Chantal to pick them up. They cruised past tall cliffs on their right where people had gathered, some of them pointing at their yacht.

"You guys, come here," she called over her shoulder. "Come look at this."

Fiona stepped up beside her, fussing with the neckline of her top. "Did I get the right top? This thing feels a little small for me. Does yours fit right?"

"What? Oh." She was surprised to see that Fiona's pearl blue top was open nearly to her navel. "That's what this is for," she said, handing Fi a roll of body tape she'd found on the bed. Fiona's mouth hung open.

Kiki snagged the roll out of her fingers. "It's double sticky, see?" She stripped off a piece and tucked it inside Fiona's top where it gaped away from her breast, then pressed the fabric against it.

Kiki's outfit was revealing, too, but on her it looked perfectly natural. She leaned against the railing and gave Zoey bored eyeroll. "What are you on about?"

She sounded impatient, like the Kiki she'd first met. Zoey shrugged. "Nothing. I just wanted you to see." She gave a prom queen wave at the people who waved at them.

Fiona quit fidgeting and grabbed hold of the rail. "It's the Cabrillo Monument," she said with conviction.

"And you know this because?" Zoey asked.

"I picked up some brochures at the reception desk when we were checking in." Fiona flitted back to the table by the sofa and scooped them up, then sorted through the stack and pulled one out. "See? It commemorates Juan Rodriguez Cabrillo, the first European to set foot in the country in 1542," she read with her usual enthusiasm. "There's a lighthouse up there too, and some tide pools on the other side of the peninsula." She fanned out the brochures. "There's lots of stuff to do here. San Diego looks amazing."

Zoey glanced at the brochures briefly, then turned her attention back to dusty-green, brush-covered cliffs that reminded her a little of the dry season at home. "I doubt we'll get a chance to get off this boat or do anything without Flora while we're here."

Fiona slumped a little. "I know, but I can dream, can't I? At least, I hope we can get out of our rooms and explore this boat."

Her eyes took on the wistful quality that reminded Zoey so much of her friend, Shuda. She missed her even more knowing it was likely she would never see her again.

She lifted her gaze to what the brochure map showed as Point Loma, pushing down a little lump of regret as they cruised by, increasing their speed. Leaving your friends was just a part of leaving home. It couldn't be helped. But it felt like the further they sailed away from the point, the more a part of her was fading away.

The view was spectacular though, and she let herself drift under its spell. The ocean's surface was polished in the same lemony-pink glow as the coming sunset on the horizon, so calm it was difficult to tell where the water ended and the sky began.

On reflex, she ran her fingers along the gold chain at her neck, picked up the coin, and held it tight. For a moment she felt as though she'd stepped into an embrace so full of love and permanence that nothing could take it away. A wave of calm washed over her, easing the ache in her heart, the same way it had when she'd rested her hands on the dolphins.

She gave Fiona's hand a squeeze. "Of course you can dream, Fi," she murmured. "I mean, who would have thought two weeks ago we'd be here on this fancy yacht? I certainly didn't see it coming and people say I have the gift of *sight*."

Fiona recovered her cheerful smile. "Huh," she said, thoughtfully. "I bet those people who waved at us from the monument wished they were on this yacht."

Kiki pressed her lips tight, fixing a serious gaze on Fiona. "Just make sure you don't mess up your tumbling in rehearsal or Flora will have you walking the plank."

*   *   *

Zoey blotted her face with a towel as they left the empty salon after dress rehearsal. "You're run was great, by the way," she told Fiona, feeling like she needed to buoy her up after Kiki's remarks earlier. Fiona did, however, look a little green around the gills.

"Take your seasick pills," Zoey said, shaking one of the pills from an envelope Chantal had left them, along with some juices to replace their fluids. To Zoey's delight, the feel of the waves under the boat, like being pressed back against the seat during takeoff, only exhilarated her. However, thinking about tonight's actual performance made goosebumps rise like porcupine quills all over her skin.

It was one thing to dance a recital in front of the parents of all the dancers and a few senior citizens and city arts promoters at the little theater in Gaborone; they were about to dance in front of a group of strangers on an obscenely huge yacht in the middle of the ocean on the other side of the planet from home. It was bordering on surreal. No amount of practice could prepare them for that moment, especially after what Kiki had told her. It was exhausting just thinking about it.

The couple of hours break sailed by. After a light dinner, in no time they were called to refresh their makeup and check their costumes for the actual performance. Zoey had spent the time with butterflies in her stomach and an adrenaline high. She was finally doing what she'd dreamed of all her life, right? Performing as a professional dancer? So why did it feel so wrong?

As was becoming her habit, Zoey stole a look from behind the stage curtain as the seats in the salon began to fill. The main salon of the *Josephine* was organized around cocktail tables set so close the stage, a dancer could look straight into the faces of the patrons—close enough to see heavy gold rings on their fingers, the snappy press on their trousers, tanned bodies peeking out behind open-collared shirts, and the color of their eyes.

She caught her breath when she recognized the man sitting in an upholstered booth smack in the middle of the front row. Angelica sat next to him on one side, and a girl she had seen near the reception desk when they'd boarded the yacht sat on the other. As if he could feel her eyes on him, his eyes lifted to the split in the curtain, and for a fraction of a second, it felt like he looked straight at her. A chill prickled up her spine, raising those porcupine quills again. She let go of the curtain and straightened the thin shoulder straps of her costume.

Fiona stood behind her, fidgeting with the skimpy thong at her backside. "What's the matter?"

"Nothing," Zoey said. "Break a leg, that's all." Fiona rolled her shoulders, once, then cracked her neck. "Right. You, too."

Zoey rolled up onto the balls of her feet and then back down, trying to focus her attention on her muscles. No matter what else was going on, they were dancers in a company and they each had a role to play. Zoey was sure no one was going to throw them overboard, but if they didn't do their best, she had no doubts they would get bumped out of their leading roles.

She threw a glance over at Kiki. If she was nervous, she didn't show it. Her movements were slow, deliberate, almost silken as she stretched and waited on the opposite side of the stage for her musical cue. It was clear, she had already detached from reality, escaping into the character she was about to portray. Zoey watched her with admiration and not a little jealousy, until she realized, now that she knew Victoria better, that calm detachment was a disguise. There was determination in her stance, but there was also something else. Something had changed in the time between rehearsal and show time. Zoey could see it in Kiki's eyes, a wild, almost feral gleam behind a pasted-on smile. Zoey attempted to give her a reassuring nod, but Kiki deliberately avoided her eyes.

At intermission, Flora scooted in next to Angelica in the booth at the foot of the stage. Rhalston, the man for which she had planned this entire performance had left the booth. This was her chance to check in with her client.

"So. What do you think?"

Angelica said, "Your lead, Kiki is it? She's pretty amazing. I have to say, though, Rhalston couldn't keep his eyes off that girl from Botswana." She raised her hand to get the attention of a waiter carrying a tray of champagne flutes. "He said the Victoria types were a dime a dozen. But that girl..." She lifted the program Flora had printed at the business center just before the performance and pointed at Zoey's name. "Zenobia? You say she's eighteen? She looks, I don't know. Younger. But those amber eyes and the way she moves. Rhalston was entranced. He wants to see her privately *tonight*."

Flora's face heated in a sudden flush. She had made it very clear, the girls would only be *dancing* on stage the first night. The truth was, she hadn't had time to do a proper training, having spent the extra day in Gaborone on the way to Paris. She needed to head this off. According to her sources, Rhalston would be the most likely to call the troupe back for repeat performances on his private island, an engagement that could bring huge rewards, maybe even contribute to her eventual retirement.

She had spent the hours between dress rehearsal and show time instructing Victoria on what would be expected of her after the shows. Despite the air of sultry allure the girl exuded, probably the result of living on the streets of London before she scouted her, Victoria had been more than reluctant. The usual perks--having her own suite, a luxurious wardrobe, access to alcohol, and little boosts in her refreshments--had been no enticement to comply, nor was the offer of a monetary bonus.

Flora should have known. Victoria had been close friends with Tabitha who had not only proved to be an embarrassment but put Flora in a position she'd hoped never to repeat. Once a girl was on the inside, there was no safe way to let her go.

Yet here she was, resorting to tactics that could prove difficult down the line. Her mouth went dry at the thought. The truth was, she wasn't sure threatening Victoria's friends, Zoe and Fiona would be sufficient to bring the girl around. Flora had done her best to lay out the terms of her position. "It would behoove you to be a little more… *flexible*, my dear," she had advised the girl. "You may never get a chance like this again." Victoria had been adamant. "And what if I don't sit in this pervert's lap for you? Are your going to drug me and get rid of me like you did Tabitha?"

The sass and the image it had evoked made Flora angry, but it also gave her pause. It was one thing to pay a stagehand to drug a girl and leave her in a London alley, quite another to dispose of someone aboard a vessel in the middle of the ocean.

She pushed hard at the memory of what had happened to Tabitha, shaking off a sharp pang of guilt. She was getting too old for this business.

But now, with Rhalston's interest in Zoe, she had a possible solution. Zoey had come from rough circumstances, a willing runaway who wouldn't want to be sent home. She might be willing to push beyond her comfort zone to reach her goals. And from what she'd seen, Zoey was more sympathetic to her friends. She would find it more difficult to ignore a threat to their safety.

Flora needed time to sort this out.

"Oh, my goodness, tonight is absolutely out of the question. The girls are already exhausted from jet lag," she said, hedging. She sipped her champagne, trying to look casual. "Their performance has been a little off tonight and we've still got the second half to go."

Angelica lifted a shoulder. "They looked magnificent to me and Rhalston was transfixed."

Flora stood and gave her a wide smile. "Wonderful. Then he will be really impressed tomorrow night." She turned and made her way through the tables before Rhalston could return and press his case.

Jamal let himself flow with the cadence of Tessa's voice--slow and smooth, methodically relaxing his body starting with his toes and working his way to his head. He had been a little anxious at first once they'd made the decision to let him try hypnosis to ask for a vision. What if he saw something completely different? Or saw something even more disturbing than before? What if he was too late to save his sister? What if he got lost in time and never found his way back? What if… What if he couldn't be hypnotized at all?

He stirred a moment as the sound of motorcycles on Marine Avenue interrupted the quiet.

"Just let it go, let them pass," Tessa crooned. Her voice was like a smooth caress, settling him deeper as she spoke. "If you hear them again, they won't disturb you. Now let the backs of your hands rest against the floor. They are heavy now."

His breathing slowed, his hands melted into the floor, his anxiety drifted away like sea foam. *Why had he never tried this before? Everybody should try this.*

As if seeing his concentration drift, Tessa reeled him back in. "Focus on the connection with your sister, Jamal."

She was right. If he wanted to help his sister, he would need to stay on task. He pressed his coin between his thumb and forefinger; the Serpent's coil resting loosely at his wrist. It was the two working together that took him to the yacht the first time. He hoped it would work again.

"How are you feeling?" Tessa prompted, her voice soft and slow.

"Um... Gooooood..." His tongue felt like a sea slug in his mouth.

Lexi pressed her hand on his shoulder. "He's under," he heard her say as if she were in another room.

"Okay," Tessa's voice hovered somewhere in the ether around him. "Let's move on to the next step. Remember what I told you. If at any time you don't like what's happening, or you feel out of control, all you have to do is lift a finger, and I'll count you back home like we practiced. Okay?"

He nodded.

"Now take another deep breath and focus on being with your sister. Remember how it made you feel... She was a part of you, and... "

Their bodies were suspended in a warm, weightless calm, their tiny hearts beating as one, safe in the undefinable whoosh and murmur of their private world. The lifelong feeling he was never alone.

"Now, think of something you really like to do," Tessa said, her voice slow and methodical. "Just let that feeling take over. Tell me when you're there."

What he liked was floating weightless underwater, drifting among the fronds of a seaweed forest over a sandy bottom teaming with life. He lifted his finger. It was all he could manage.

"Okay, Jamal. Go find your sister."

He breathed in and out slowly, the way he did on a dive as he followed *Salacia's* anchor rope, one hand over the other, taking him to the bottom of a sandy reef…

∗　　　∗　　　∗

A woman of a commanding stature stood with her back to him in a courtyard, a firm breeze stirred heavy skirts about her ankles.

"Leave us," she ordered a servant. The servant released a pair of children she'd led into the courtyard, then bowed, backing away.

The woman stood tall, erect with the bearing of a queen; her skin a burnished ivory, wide set almond eyes. Her lips full and set with determination. Half of her oiled, blue-black hair was braided with strands of gemstone and gold beads and piled high atop her head, the rest of the bejeweled strands spilled over her shoulders, long and thick.

Her jaw was set like the stone around them--strong, firm, impenetrable. They stood on a stone diaz, stone columns supported a curved colonnade, stone bricks created stone walls.

A man in a short tunic the color of the dirt under his worn sandals lit sconces along a colonnade leading from the diaz to an ornate iron gate.

Jamal swallowed hard on a dry throat. Anxiety tightened the muscles in his chest. This was definitely not the scene he had visited before. He was holding his breath and he let it out slowly as he'd practiced with Tessa. Observe. Wait. See what happens.

The woman watched the man with the torch as he made his way to the gate. When the last sconce was lit, he turned, sent her a brief nod, then slipped out of sight.

Wow! This was radical! It was like his compound back in Bole. High walls protected them from intruders, but also held them captive. Only he was pretty sure this wasn't his time. It was a long time ago. From what he could tell, it wasn't even this century. There would be no motorcycles rumbling outside these walls anytime soon. His shoulders drooped in disappointment. Despite all their rehearsing, he had gone the wrong direction. But it was cool. Way cool. His pulse quickened, excitement sparking in his belly. Tessa's words echoed in his head.

Breathe.

Breathe.

Breathe.

The muscles in his chest relaxed until, with a swish of her skirt and the faint scent of roses…

…the woman turned and gazed directly at him. He looked behind him a moment but there was no one else there. She saw him, and just that quick, he was THERE.

She grabbed his shoulders and, *whoa*, he felt the strength in her grip. Her eyes, luminous green and lined in dark kohl, locked onto his and he realized, he must be looking out of the boy's eyes. His heart thumped hard. This was… weird.

Even more weird, he thought, dragging in a ragged breath, he recognized the woman. It was the lady embossed on the front of his coin. No doubt about it. He had done his homework, researched the coin and everything he could find about the queen. She was missing her crown and the ornate vest and belts shown in the Schmaltz painting, *Last Look at Palmyra*, but there was no doubt in his mind. He was locked in the gaze of the warrior Queen Zenobia, which put him somewhere in the third century, modern era.

Her hands clamped him by the shoulders, pulling him back into her world. Those eyes burned into his, drilling into his soul. "Who are you?" she demanded, giving his shoulders a shake.

Jamal panted, shaking his head. "Your son?" he offered, not sure what to say. If he was only an observer, why did he feel her hands bearing down on him like a pair of claws? How did he feel her fury?

She glared into his eyes another long moment, her brows narrowing on him.

Holy crap! She'd made him. An intruder. Somebody she wasn't expecting. Now what?

He started to take a step back but she caught him again and held him firm. It was then he saw them. The pair of golden snakes coiled at her wrists. Just like the ones in Tessa's workshop.

"Stay where you are, young man," she ordered pointing a long finger at him. Jamal huffed out a nervous laugh. Inside he was fifteen-year-old Jamal who had his shit together, but outside, he was only a five-year-old boy. He could not have moved if his life depended on it. In fact, at that moment by the look in her eyes, he had every reason to believe that it did.

And then, like turning a page in a book, the energy shifted and her expression softened to that of a concerned mother. She let go of him with one arm and included the little girl who had been standing next to him into her embrace. Their eyes met and it was as though he'd been struck by lightning. The girl's face was a mirror image of his own. Almond eyes the color of olive leaves, Nubian nose, gold studs at her ears, her skin full shades darker than their mother's. His head was shaved close, her hair, twisted in tight rows over her head, hung in a thick braid at her back; but other than that she could be his reflection. It was her. But... *how?*

Zenobia pushed them to arm's length a moment, looking them both up and down with fierce love in her eyes. "Listen to me, my children. We don't have much time."

The girl started to whimper and Zenobia gave her a quick hug. "None of that now, my love."

Feeling the little girl's fear, he slipped his hand into hers and squeezed until she settled.

There was a commotion outside the gate. Zenobia hurried them to the back of the diaz nearest the domicile. A pair of lapis-lazuli dolphins sprang from a fountain, showering water from their beaks into a large scallop shell. Jamal put his hand out, letting the cool stream run through his fingers. His sister followed his example. A moment later, their mother turned them away from the dolphins and knelt down to bring herself to eye level with them. She took their hands in hers, joining them in a circle.

"Today, you will embark on a new adventure." She gave their hands a squeeze. "We will not be together again, after this day."

The little girl cried out, "No!"

Zenobia lifted the child's chin with a crooked finger. "Gaius has given you your freedom, my love. This is a precious gift."

"But I don't want that gift," the girl cried. "Don't make us go."

Zenobia shook her head. The sadness he saw in her eyes said this decision couldn't have been her choice. "It is the way of your world now. You have each other. That will have to be enough."

Her voice came as an echo, before it circled back to his ears.

"I see you my son," she said, "Now and forever you are bound to your sister."

Her eyes shifted to the girl's. "And you my love, are bound to your brother. No matter where your paths lead, you will have this connection." She let her eyes linger on his once more, searing the meaning into his soul, then did the same with his sister.

And then, at her command, the bracelets circling each of her wrists slithered from hers to their own like a living things.

The instant the serpents crossed over, Zenobia broke away, lifted her arms to the heavens' and threw her head back.

Jamal shaded his eyes against blinding flash of pure blue energy that Zenobia seemed to pull right out of the sky. It swirled around her body before it condensed and then possessed her.

She turned to face them. Blue lightning flashed from her hands and spun out around them, like the serpent's coils circling their wrists, binding them together.

When the energy subsided, the serpent's coil warmed to his skin, tightened, then slithered up his arm and embedded itself around his biceps. Eyes wide, he flashed a look to his sister who reached to touch the one at her own arm. Understanding settled in. It was done. In that moment they were no longer children. They would go forward into their lives without their mother. They had no choice in the matter.

Zenobia commanded their attention once more. "Wherever you travel in this world or the next, keep these with you and never let them go. They carry with them a piece of my soul, my power. If you are ever separated, they are imbued with the power, indeed, the mandate to reunite any who bear my blood."

The gate at the far end of the compound burst open. His sister's eyes flew open. Horses, men and carts thundered through, dust clouds rising behind them. The man who had lit torches earlier drove a cart out to meet them loaded with all their worldly possessions and a covered shelter at the back.

Gaius strolled behind, his jaw set, a tight smile on his lips, his eyes on Zenobia. "Let it never be said, I failed to keep my word." He added two heavy wooden trunks to the cart, hitting the planks with a jingle of coins.

The little girl began to cry in earnest as one of the soldiers strode toward her.

Rising to his full height, jaw set in determination, the boy strode forward to intercept the soldier. He held out his hand to his sister, and together they took their places on the cart.

CHAPTER 15 - YOU CAN DO THIS

Off the Port of San Diego, 2019

Zoey's nerves melted away the moment she stepped out on stage. She was immersed in the lights, the costumes, the music, and the exhilarating freedom of the dance. She kept her focus, didn't look at the crowd, just danced her heart out, buoyed by her love of movement and whatever was in that juice Flora had given them before the performance. Zoey could have danced all night.

She had never felt so free, that is, until they were escorted back to their rooms and Kiki pulled she and Fiona into her private suite, her beautiful face hardened into a mask of worry.

"What happened? What's wrong?" Zoey stiffened in anticipation.

Fiona wiped perspiration from her hair line in the crook of her arm. "Oh my gosh, you didn't love that, Kiki? Did you hear that crowd? They *loved* us!"

She did chest roll, ending on a punchy hip walk around the room. Zoey reached out and touched Fiona's arm, unable to take her eyes from Kiki's face. "Sh-h-h-h... What is it Victoria?"

Kiki ghosted to her windows, her back to them. "It's not safe here you guys." She turned around, gripping the curtains. "I was going to tell you we had to get away from Flora when we got back to shore, but... we can't wait."

Zoey and Fiona slipped in beside her. Together they looked out over the black water. There wasn't one light from shore anywhere in sight.

"They want us for sex," Kiki said. "That's what this is all about." She lifted her eyes to Zoey's, a tear spilled over her cheek. "Those old, fat rich guys in that audience tonight? They were sampling the menu, placing their orders... "

"But that's gross!" Fiona said. "Flora wouldn't... "

"She would," Kiki said. "She did! I knew it when we left London. Tabitha refused to go along and she got rid of her!"

"She's right, Fi," Zoey added.

"But why didn't you tell me before?" Fiona questioned, glancing back and forth between them.

Kiki traced a circle on the floor with a pointed toe. "We didn't want to worry you. I... I was so caught up with the idea of moving into the lead, I wanted to believe Tabs left on her own. But deep down, I knew."

Zoe felt her own stab of guilt. Hadn't she had some of those same thoughts?

"Anyway, tonight," Kiki went on, her eyes still fixed on her feet, "before the dress rehearsal, Flora pulled me aside, took me to her room. Told me what was expected of me, of all of us, eventually." She lifted her eyes to theirs now, her beautiful face twisted in pain. "I refused. Told her she was nothing but a scummy, low life pimp. She was so arrogant, she just laughed at me. She had a briefcase full of cash, you guys. F-U-L-L. She took out a bundle of what looked like hundreds and shoved it into my hands. Shoved it like it was nothing to her. She was so used to having piles of it, she could just toss it at me like it was nothing. Said I was no better than her. That I'd learn. But, I refused her. Told her to go *fuck* herself, I wasn't going to ruin myself for some rich or geezer just because he had enough money to party on some private yacht."

"What did she do?" Zoey asked, afraid to hear the answer.

"She laughed at me. Laughed! She said I would do exactly as she said, or you and Fiona would suffer." Tears spilled over her cheeks and hung off her chin. She wiped them away.

Fiona shook her head slowly. "But, that just can't be. She said she was here to protect us. To take care of us. She... "

Zoey took hold of Fiona's shoulders "Look at me, Fiona. Listen. She groomed us. The Dance troupe was just her cover. Her lure." Images of the day she'd first met Flora at the recital in Gaborone sifted through her mind. "She crooned and fawned over me, complemented me, and read me like a book. I was ripe for the picking, just like you, Fi. I couldn't wait to get away from home. I was flattered, and full of myself. Flora had me believing I could join her company and dance my way to a new life, I could win a leading role, I could... "

They heard loud voices. Someone was coming down the hall, Flora's recognizable laugh, a man's agreeable reply.

"Oh my god," Kiki hissed. "They can't find you here." She opened the sliding glass doors to the balcony and hustled them outside, then pulled the curtains half closed to hide them.

Zoey and Fi huddled together in the corner of the balcony down behind an upholstered chaise longue. They couldn't see into the room, but they could hear the conversation.

"I thought you understood I was interested in that Zenobia girl," a man said. Zoey knew exactly who it was. The man with the pale gray eyes who had been watching her since they boarded the ship.

"Sometimes we have to wait for the things we want most," Flora crooned. "Zenobia hasn't been through *training*," she went on. "And Victoria here... well, the girls all have a bit of jet lag... "

The man's footsteps approached the balcony curtains. Zoey flattened against the deck, pressing Fiona beneath her.

"Sometimes…," he began, mocking Flora's tone, "the inexperienced ones are the best."

Zoey shivered and held Fiona close. Then they heard their friend, Kiki--tall, beautiful, brave Kiki--make what could turn out to be the biggest mistake of her life.

"And sometimes," Kiki announced, "a pedophile gets exactly what he deserves." They heard a sharp thump, then a man yelped and cursed. Zoe guessed Kiki had stomped his foot.

"How dare you," Flora said low, her words full of contempt. There was a sharp slap of flesh striking flesh. Then Kiki cried out, and something heavy hit the floor.

"And you call yourself a professional," the man accused. His footsteps stalked toward the balcony, then stopped a moment. Zoey could hear his heavy breathing; she clamped her hand over her own mouth willing him to go away. At last, his footsteps retreated. She let her breath out slowly, looking into Fiona's wide eyes.

"Oh, my god," Flora keened, fear replacing contempt in her voice. "Victoria, honey. You're okay. You're okay."

There was a low moan. It was obvious Kiki was not okay. Zoey felt a sickening ache in her heart.

"Send me that Botswana girl," the man said, as if nothing unusual had happened. Zoey seethed with anger, shook with it. It was all she could do not to rush him herself and gouge out his eyes.

"Kiki. Kiki?" came Flora's voice again. "You're okay, baby. Look at me."

There was no response.

Kiki was not okay.

"Well. Don't just stand there, Rhalston. Call Angelica," she ordered.

Heavy footsteps retreated across the room, then the door latch opened. "Not my job," Rhalston said, and the heavy door clicked shut.

Zoey's chest heaved. It would be foolish to charge into the room, but she couldn't hold herself back any longer, she rose, tiptoed to the sliding door, and peeked around the curtain.

Kiki lay on the floor, blood staining the front of her costume, a gash over her forehead. Flora cradled her in her arms, rocking back and forth, as smudge of blood below the cap sleeves of her gown, black mascara leaving trails down her cheeks. She slowly lowered Kiki's body to the floor, retrieved her bag from the console table by the door, and retrieved her phone.

"Angel," she said, obviously holding back a sob, "I need you in Victoria's suite. *Now.*"

Zoey and Fiona waited on the balcony, barely able to breathe until Angelica and two of her helpers lifted Kiki's rag doll body off the floor and carried her out of the suite. It was a miracle none of them had thought to check in on the other girls. Still holding each other up, they stole across the hall into their suite and threw the security latch.

Zoey could not stop her body's shaking.

Fiona sobbed. "Do you think she's going to be all right?"

Zoe shook her head. "I don't know. There was so much blood."

"Maybe we could find some of those SOS flares like they used on the Titanic."

Zoey pictured the tiny Titanic on a massive sea, the flares disappearing unseen in the night. Would they be seen twelve miles offshore? She doubted it. She pinched her gold coin between her fingers, her eyes squeezed shut. *What should we do?* She waited a beat, but that old sense of abandonment hollowed out in her chest. It was as though the boy in her dreams had abandoned her, too. She had never felt so empty, so raw, so alone.

Fiona sniffed and straightened, taking on a determination Zoe hadn't seen in her before. "One thing for sure, we can't get off the boat until we get back to the harbor. We've gotta play this thing out. Tell the other girls."

"No," Zoey snapped, reality of their situation closing in. "That will just put all of us in danger. It's *me* he wants." She paced across their suite, running her fingers through her tight curls. I'll just do what he says."

She stood in front of the dolphin statue now, gathering her courage. "We'll have to play like we don't know or they'll have to get rid of us, too. In the meantime, we need a plan. Even if we get off the boat, then what? We have no money, no clothes, Flora has our passports. We're screwed."

She ran cold, sweaty palms up and down her thighs.

Fiona cocked her hands at her hips, a devilish light in her eyes. "Our passports are fake. Useless. But I can probably get us money. Cash. Flora doesn't keep it in the safe. Doesn't trust the staff. Kiki told us. Heaps of cash in her briefcase."

"What? You think you can just stroll into Flora's room and grab a briefcase full of cash?"

"We'll, maybe not stroll right in. And we don't need all of it, right? Just enough to get us away from this boat and notify the authorities."

"What authorities? Fi, we don't know anything about this place."

Fiona slapped the pile of brochures off the console table next to the dolphins, shuffled through. "There's the Harbor Patrol, for starters," she said, throwing down a tall postcard brochure, "and then there's the friggin' United States Navy." She threw down another brochure about the U.S.S. Midway Museum.

Zoey huffed out a breath, a fresh surge of hope pumping through her veins. She may not have dream boy on her side anymore, but they had each other and Fiona was right. She picked up the pile, shuffled through, scanning the titles, trying to gather her thoughts until an image on one of them took her breath away. Her fingers went reflexively to the coin at her necklace. She dropped the brochure on the table and backed away.

"What?" Fiona stepped up to retrieve the brochure, her brows knitting as she scanned the photo. An then she saw it. She stabbed her finger at the boy in the photo. "Oh my god, Zoe, this guy could be--"

"My twin," Zoey whispered, her face going cold. That boy. That boy on the ship she'd seen in her visions. Was it really him? Or was it just wishful thinking? Her imagination? She squeezed the coin tight between her fingers. Could this be what this all came down to?

She snatched the brochure back and opened it, spread it out on the table. There was no question about it. It was *him*. The boy she had come to know as a brother. Standing with a group of teens around the deck of a dive boat, each of them fitted out in dive suits. The glint of a gold coin gleaming on his chest.

Her knees went to liquid, dropping her slowly to the floor.

This boy, this twin. Her brother. She'd been sensing his presence all her life. It couldn't be a coincidence that right now, when she and Fiona faced what was the scariest moment of their lives, this boy who looked uncannily like herself showed up on a brochure in her own hands?

Fiona dropped down to sit beside her on the floor, the brochure in her hand. "This boat? The *Salacia*? It says there's a diving adventure launching from a visitors dock in San Diego Harbor. Wait. What day is it?" She looked up at Zoey, her green eyes shining with excitement.

Zoey suddenly realized how out of touch with reality she had let herself get. "I... I don't know. How lame is that?"

"Angelica left a schedule on the kitchenette bar." She sailed across the room and scooped it up. "Tonight was our first performance, so, it's Friday, right? September second." She scanned the brochure. "The first excursion on this *Salacia* voyage is... next weekend. You have to have reservations.

There's a number here. And a website. This could be our way out. It's an omen. I mean, the guy looks just like you. That has to be a sign."

Zoe gripped the coin tighter and leaned her head back against the couch, adrenaline zipping through her, making her fingertips tingle. It was more than a sign. But how was she going to explain it to Fi? She'd deliberately kept her visions to herself since she'd left Botswana. What good had telling anyone ever gotten her?

Fiona broke into a wider smile, the tears drying on tracks they'd made through her make up. "So that's it. We get into Flora's room, take some of her money, not enough so she'd notice, then when the ship docks, we break away from the group and find this *Salacia*."

"Right. And in the meantime, I lose my virginity to some fat cat who doesn't give a damn about you or me?"

Fiona dropped the brochures and stalked to the kitchen, yanked a Coke from the fridge, and pished it open. "Maybe you can stall him. Stomp him like Kiki did."

Zoey ran her hands over the cool lapiz on the backs of the dolphins. She doubted Rhalston would fall for that one twice. "No. Yeah. Maybe. Let's get undressed. Flora's got to be pretty shaken up about Kiki. She'll be by to check up on us. We have to act like we don't know anything. In the meantime, I need to think this through."

They didn't have long to wait. No sooner had they showered and climbed into their respective beds when the knock came at the door.

"Girls?" Flora's voice came through the crack in the door. "I thought I told you not to throw this latch."

Zoe got out of bed and padded to the door, let Flora in. Gone were the mascara smudges, replaced by freshly applied makeup. "Is Fiona awake, too? I need to talk to both of you."

Concern wrinkled Flora's brow, but Zoe didn't trust her anymore. "Fi. Flora wants to talk."

Fiona joined them, sitting on the sofa, sporting a smile Zoey knew was hard to manage considering all they had witnessed only an hour before. She was stronger than she looked.

Flora sat in the chair opposite the sofa. "So. Victoria's had a little accident."

Little accident, my butt. Zoey wanted to strangle Flora, but she held herself back.

At the girls' feigned surprise, Flora raised her hand. "She's all right. Just sprained an ankle in the show. But, as you might guess, she won't be at rehearsal tomorrow and it's likely, maybe not for the rest of this trip. It is... unfortunate."

Zoey's heart shrank into a cold little ball in the center of her chest. She knew what was coming. She was going to get exactly what she wanted. It should have made her happy. Instead, it made her sick to her stomach. She sat on her hands to keep from wringing them in her lap.

"So, you, Zoey," Flora went on as if she were announcing Christmas was coming early, "will take her place in the show tomorrow."

Zoey's response knotted in her throat. Fiona stood, covered for her. "Can we see Kiki?" Her eyes flicked to Zoey's then back to Flora. "She must be really disappointed."

Flora must have been prepared for this, for she didn't bat an eye. "Like I said, she's going to be fine, but they've got her in the ship's infirmary and it's small, so they don't allow visitors."

She stood and held out her arms like she was bestowing a gift. "As my A team, you two will move into the one and two positions. I know I can count on you."

Zoe and Fi exchanged worried glances.

"Which means, we'll be moving you, Zoe, into your own suite."

Zoey pressed her lips together, then forged ahead. "I... don't need all the fuss. Why don't we leave the rooming situation the way it is for now? If Kiki's ankle is better in the morning... she'll want to-
-"

Kind Flora disappeared, replaced by the woman Zoe had heard in Kiki's room. "You think you know better than me? That you're smart enough to run this show, *Roshana*? Make my decisions for me? For the ship's doctor?"

Flora emphasized Zoey's real name, reminding her where she'd come from. It brought their situation into sharp focus. They had essentially been kidnapped, and if they didn't do exactly as they were told, they'd wind up like Tabitha, and now, Kiki.

Flora stalked to the door, grabbed hold of the handle in a white-knuckle grip and turned around. "Stay here tonight since you're already bedded down. We'll move you tomorrow during rehearsal."

She let herself out and Zoey hurried to throw the latch in defiance. She leaned her back against the door and let out her breath. How stupid she had been to think all the travel, the clothes, the luxury surrounding them came without a price. Now Fiona and Kiki's safety was in her hands. She was beginning to think giving in to her cousin would have been a better option.

Fiona took her by the hand, peeled her away from the door and her misery, then pushed her toward the bedroom. "That was close, Zoey, but were still together, at least for now. Tell me about your plan."

Zoe shook her head, the stark reality of their situation sinking in. "I don't know yet. But whatever it is, we've got to do it before rehearsal in the morning."

Zoe lay awake for hours and still, her plan was only half baked. There was nothing she could do shut up in this room. She needed to explore the yacht before there was a chance Flora or Chantal would be up. She stole out of bed, dressed, and plumped pillows under the covers on her bed.

"What are you doing?" Fiona's voice was clogged with sleep. She leaned over to see the digital clock. "It's four friggin' a.m. why are you *uuuuuup?*"

Zoe straightened, a sudden rush of guilt heated her face. She was hoping to get this done without Fiona getting involved.

"I'm just thinking." She'd let Kiki get injured. She wasn't about to risk Fiona getting hurt as well. "Go back to sleep."

Fiona sat up. She nodded to Zoey's faked presence in the bunk. "That doesn't look like thinking to me. That looks like sneaking out."

Zoe blew out a long breath then sat next to her friend, twisting her hair into a tight knot on top of her head. "First, I'm going to try to find Kiki. Then, I'm going to check out the rest of the boat. There's got to be a way to get off this thing. In an emergency, you know? Maybe we can--"

Fiona threw off the covers. "I'm coming with you."

"No! One of us has got to answer if Flora or Chantal knocks on our door."

Fiona frowned, slumped, dragged the covers up around her, looking more like a ruffled street urchin than the talented acrobatic flier she was. "You're right. But listen, I have an idea, too."

Zoe pulled on her jeans, shuffled around her bunk until she found her shoes. Her mind had been churning with worry about the *training* that was sure to come before their second performance. If what had happened to Kiki was any indication, she wouldn't have much choice about what was expected of her. She was hoping to find a solution without putting Fiona in jeopardy, but the time for that had passed.

"I'm listening." She bent over, slipped on her shoes.

"Okay. So, I wait until the last possible minute before tonight's performance for Flora to leave her cabin, then rush to the door and tell her I lost my body tape, which is, uh, true, but..." She waved the digression away. "Never mind that. Anyway, I'll be all desperate, because, um, I am, and I won't stop until she lets me *in*. She'll do it because she's impatient that way, right? And I'll remind her the doors lock automatically, so she won't have to worry I'll leave her room open to burglars." She giggled at herself then.

Zoe nodded, rolled her hand to push Fi forward.

"Then, I'll tape the door jam, so I can come back during intermission and take the money out of her briefcase." She sat back, satisfied with herself. "All you have to do is keep Flora busy during intermission."

"Fi, I can't let you do that. It's too dangerous."

Fiona scowled at her. "Look. I know you and Kiki think I'm just a silly kid. You forget I was living on the streets in Dublin when Flora picked me up."

Zoe shot her arms through her sweatshirt sleeves, flipped up the hood to cover her hair. "I don't know, Fi. There's too many ways it could go wrong."

"Have you got a better idea?" Fi prompted, imitating Zoey's impatient hand roll. "*Cuz*, it's already gone wrong. Kiki got hurt, bad. We don't even know where she is, and now the same thing could happen to you if we don't do something."

Zoey moved to the balcony doors. "You're right, Fi. But we have to be careful."

"Careful? Zoey, they could actually throw us overboard and get away with it. Our IDs are fake. They changed my name before I ever left London. Nobody but Flora and Chantal know we're here. This yacht? Those men out there?" She lifted her chin toward the door. "You think they're going to blow the whistle on Flora if a couple of girls go missing? No. This whole operation is illegal and they'd be in a lot of trouble, too if they did."

Zoey swallowed hard. Fiona was right. It was past time to be careful. They needed to do whatever it took to get off this boat.

Fi was not letting it go. "Kiki is my friend, too. You don't have to protect me. I can do this. I have to try. I can't just sit here and let this all happen."

She was right again. Zoey couldn't do this alone. If they were going to get themselves and Kiki off this damn boat, it would take both of them to get the job done. *And*, they had to get off alive if they were going to blow the whistle on these scums and save the rest of the girls.

"Okay. So, let's say you get that done. I can keep Flora occupied during the intermission. Act like I'm stoked, like I'm all into the lead, will do whatever it takes, you know?" It had been a nice dream while it lasted. She would have to deal with Rhalston no matter what happened. "It will help me to know you make it back okay before that final dance."

"I'll give you the thumbs up when I get back, Right?"

"Right." She zipped up her hoodie and went silently to the door. "I'm going to the ship's infirmary. We know Flora's lying about Kiki. If she's not in the infirmary, I need to find out where she is.

We can't leave her here, Fi. We have to find a way to get her off the boat, too."

*　　　*　　　*

It hadn't been that hard to find the infirmary. She'd made her way along the main deck toward the yacht's stern where she'd run into a night watchman, faked a turned ankle, and he'd escorted her there himself.

The ship's doctor looked her up and down. "Aren't you supposed to be with your keeper, missy? That Chantal woman?"

"I didn't want to disturb her." Zoe rubbed her ankle, sneaking a sideways look at him. He was a doctor. That Hippocratic oath and all? Maybe she could confide in him, enlist his help. She wasn't sure. If he knew Chantal was their keeper, he might know *everything*. Better that she didn't let down her guard. At least, not until she found Kiki.

"If Chantal or Flora know I'm injured, they'll put someone else in the lead." She glanced at him again to gage his reaction.

"Dancers," he said under his breath. The look he gave her said it hadn't been the first time he'd heard those words. He motioned her to sit up on an examining table. She made the appropriate flinches and groans while he poked and prodded her ankle. "How did this happen?"

"What? Oh, I... just landed funny. Like the girl last night."

He shot her a confused look, gave her ankle a gentle twist. "Last night? What girl?"

"Ow. Yeah. You know. The girl Flora brought in here last night, after the performance? She twisted *her* ankle."

Confusion knitted his brow. "I don't remember one of you girls coming in last night."

Right. Because they never brought her here to begin with. Or, he was lying.

"Ah. Well. Good. Maybe it wasn't that bad," she said, a little louder than necessary. It was true the infirmary was small. If Kiki was there, maybe she would hear her and call out, or make a sound to let her know she was there. Zoey let the silence play out, but heard nothing. No indication that anyone else was in the infirmary.

"So what do you think? It's okay to dance on it, right?"

"It doesn't look bad," he said. "I could give you something for pain if it gives you any trouble."

"Sure," she said absently. "That would be good. And please, don't tell Miss Flora I was here."

He lifted his gaze to hers and in that moment, she knew she couldn't trust him. If what they figured was true--the *Joesephine* was being used to traffic young girls for sex--he had to have known exactly what was going on and chose to look the other way or he'd have already blown the whistle on them.

With a slight tick at the corners of his eyes, he broke their visual connection as if he could read her mind. Shoulders slumped, he ambled down a short hallway toward a locked cabinet, zipped a key from a belt holder and twisted it in the lock. Zoey imagined the weight of his oath bore down on him like a heavy stone.

Zoey tested out standing on the foot, thinking, *You'll go down with the rest of them, if I can help it, Doctor.*

She fake limped along the row of curtained beds toward the exit. It was exactly what she'd feared. Flora had lied. The ship's doctor had never seen Kiki; or if he had, he wasn't going to admit it. If Kiki was still on the boat, she was hidden away where no one could see her injuries, or worse. She refused to let herself think about that.

Near the exit, the doctor gave her a small envelope of anti-inflammatory gels. "The injury isn't serious as far as I can tell, but if it swells or you see bruising, you come back to see me, okay?"

"Yeah. Thanks." Zoey tucked the envelope into her hoodie pocket and slipped out the door.

The rest of her early morning excursion didn't yield much. There were four inflatables at the back of the yacht, but there was no way the girls could launch one without help from the crew. There was a metal box marked *Flares*, but it was locked. There was a heavy plastic bin full of life jackets they could possibly hide among for a short period of time. Otherwise, it was clear, the main transport on and off the boat when it wasn't dockside was the helicopter chocked on its pad at the foredeck. No way were they stowing away on that. It was barely big enough for a pilot and four passengers, let alone three girls, one of them badly injured.

Dejected, she'd made her way back to the cabin and crawled into her bed without a clue what to do next. Even if Fi was successful getting the money, they'd have to find a way to get by for two more nights before the boat cruised back to the harbor.

At nine a.m., Chantal showed up with breakfast buns, pushing them to get to practice since they'd all been moved into different positions. Fiona and Zoe barely spoke to each other, instead concentrating on their new moves.

Zoe returned to their cabin just before lunch to find a new key and a note that her things had been moved into her own suite across the hall. When she opened the door, Flora was there waiting for her.

Heat poured off Zoe's body from the heavy practice session. What she wanted was to stand under the shower and let the sweat sluice off her body. Instead, Flora insisted they talk immediately. It took every ounce of Zoey's resolve not to lose her shit, rush Flora, and squeeze the life out of her. She could do it, she realized in a moment of clarity. She was agile, strong, and, driven by an anger that had sparked to life the day her cousin had pinned her against the wall in her aunt's kitchen, and grown exponentially since they arrived on the yacht. But what would throttling Flora accomplish other than put Fiona and Kiki in more danger than they were already in? No. At this point, her only choice was to play the game, seem interested in whatever rewards Flora offered.

She set her shoulders with resolve, her fingers searching the comfort of the gold coin at her neck. Zenobia, her namesake, right? The Warrior queen. That had to count for something. Still, it was all she could do to hold on to a positive demeanor while listening to someone she'd trusted betray everything she'd believed. Her foot tapped uncontrollably until Flora pressed her hand on her knee.

"You're a smart girl, Zoe. I saw it the first day we met. This opportunity could turn out to be very lucrative for you."

Zoey squeezed the coin, but like before, the confidence she'd gained from her connection to the boy was somehow missing in this moment and the reality set in. She was absolutely on her own. She would do whatever it took to get her friends off this disgusting tub. She let her gaze roam around the luxury suite, hoping Flora couldn't detect the fear in her eyes.

"So, I just have one question," Zoey said, lifting her chin like she'd seen Kiki do a hundred times. "What if Kiki gets better, will she take the lead away from me? Because, that wouldn't be fair, would it?"

Flora couldn't hide a tiny tick around her mouth at the mention of Kiki before she returned a wide smile. "Oh, honey. You are a competitor after all. I was getting worried about you."

"You promised to take me away from my situation at home. And you made good on that promise. So I owe you. But, I would hate to think something as minor as a *sprained ankle* could take that all away."

Flora's eyes narrowed on hers. Zoe was pushing and she knew it, but she couldn't help herself.

"Victoria made her choices, Zoe. She had the same opportunity as you and she chose to throw it away."

"So it was more than a sprained ankle." She watched Flora unblinking, letting her words—and the fact that she didn't believe her—sink deep.

Flora shot to her feet, headed for the door. "Forget about Kiki. You just remember our little talk here tonight. Mr. Rhalston is easy to please. If he likes you, you and I will have a great future together."

Zoey followed her to the door, her steps dramatic and sensual, as if in a dance, the act feeding her strength. "And if he doesn't?"

Flora stared at her a long moment before she opened the door. "You just make sure that he *does*."

Jamal sat up on a gasp, his heart pounding so hard, he had trouble catching his breath. The serpent's coil hung loose at his wrist, and his biceps burned like before.

Lexi dropped down beside him and scooped him into her arms. "Oh my gosh, Jammers. Are you all right?"

Five pairs of wide eyes--his mother and father, Phillip and Tessa, and his grandmother--were all focused on him. He was back. "I... I'm good." He pressed his hands against his ears a moment, "I... oh. Wow, that was... "

He glanced around the room, relief opening his lungs for a full breath. He was exhausted but he wasn't terrified like before when he'd tripped on his own in Tessa's shop. His mouth was dry as the landscape he'd just left. "Can I have a drink of water? How long was I gone?"

Phillip headed for the kitchen, Tessa sat on the floor with he and his mother. "Ten, fifteen minutes at the most."

"I can't believe it. That was..." He made an explosion sound. "Crazy. Just, cray, you know?

But," he sighed, shoulders slumping, the reality hitting him hard. The experience was exhilarating, magical even, but now that he realized he was fully back, unsuccessful. "I didn't find her."

His eyes went to his mother's in apology. "I'm sorry. I just..." That breathless feeling took over again.

Lexi cupped her hands around his face. "It's all right, Jamal. Just breathe, honey, okay?"

Phil handed him a glass of water. He guzzled it down.

"I didn't find her," he said to his dad, the back of his throat aching with disappointment. "I went *back* in time. Not forward."

"Back?"

Jamal gripped the coin at his neck, his eyes went to Zaire, "Tell me about the coins. Where did grandfather find them?"

His father's brow furrowed as he studied Jamal's face. "It was a wreck, of course. In the shallows not far from Alexandria. There were no amphora to speak of, other than what mariners would take for supplies--oil, wine. No Ivory or large quantities. So we figured the vessel was inbound. Likely from Rome. We estimated by the number of metal nails we found and the coins, of course, the wreck had to have been soon after Zenobia was captured—they would have restruck those coins—sometime around 250 CE."

Jamal gripped his necklace. "And the necklaces grandad had made from the coins? They all came from the same wreck?"

"I assume so. Only a handful, but it was a significant find for him. One of the only ones that yielded actual treasure, beyond the historical value, of course."

He twisted the bracelet on his wrist, his eyes on Tessa. "And this? This bracelet was here in the house all along?"

Tessa shook her head. "It's a long story. I'm writing a story to go with my replicas when they go on sale."

He closed his eyes now, gripping the coin tight between his fingers. "The serpents were made from her coins. I saw her. How she made them. How she sent her twins home to be with their true father." He pushed up off the floor and strode to the veranda windows.

"*Who* made them, Jamal?"

He turned to face them all now, confident in what he'd seen. "Queen Zenobia. I saw her command the gods to make them. To keep her twins safe, send them home, but they... I don't think they made it. At least, not back then. Trunks of gold went to the bottom of the sea in the wreck, but the twins and the bracelets never made it home. She had a vision, saw their shipwreck on the way back to their father's homeland. I was with her. Saw her vision." He was still having trouble believing it was true.

Tessa sent him a thoughtful look. "I doubt anyone outside this room would believe your story." She gave Lexi's shoulder a squeeze. "But we absolutely do, Jamal. The serpent's coil found her way here on a winding and eventful path and has taken us along for the ride. Who knows what adventures she spawned on her quest to bring you and your sister together. But here we are." Tessa looked at each of them in turn, then focused on Jamal. "The gold cast of Zenobia coins resonates with her spell. If everything you witnessed on your *journey* is true--and given our past experience, we have no reason to doubt it--then we have to believe your visions are intended to reunite you with your sister."

Jamal's fingers tingled under the intense pressure against the coin. "Yeah. It's what I'm supposed to do. Now. Right now." He knuckled a tear out of the corner of his eye and lifted his eyes to Phillip. "Can you get me back on that website? The one with the yachts?"

Phillip blinked at him a moment, a shock of his sandy hair swinging over his eyes. Tessa rested her hand on his arm. "Of course he can," she said, and led them all next door.

Jamal sat at Tessa's kitchen table, the others closed in, the atmosphere around them fairly crackling with expectation. He clicked through dozens of pictures, each displaying some aspect of the luxury yachts available for sale or charter. Sweat broke out on his upper lip. Urgency prickled his skin. This was taking too long. He looked up at Phillip.

"So, can we skip to, like, the most expensive ones?"

"Sure. I mean, if you think... "

"We're running out of time. It's just a feeling. I've got to go with it."

Phillip sat down and did a quick search, found a site that boasted 300-plus-foot luxury vessels for long term lease. "Try this one," he said, turning the screen toward Jamal. His mom and dad stood behind him, their arms around each other's waists. He took a deep breath. He could feel his sister near. He had to be on the right track.

He had only seen three suites on a fabulous offering when he saw it. A luxury suite filled with gorgeous works of art, and there, on a table behind a blue velvet sofa was a sculpture that grabbed his attention and held it tight. He'd seen that sculpture before. He closed his eyes and forced himself to recall the scene.

And there they were, staring him right in the face. The twin lapis lazuli dolphins from Zenobia's courtyard fountain. They stood alone, no shell below, no water spurting from their mouths, but it was them. He was sure of it.

He shoved away from the table, jumped to his feet. "That's it! That's the one!"

His dad's brows drew together. "How do you know, son?"

"It's just... I just... trust me. That's the one. She's on that yacht and she's in serious danger."

Phillip spun the computer to face him. "It's the *Josephine*." He looked up at Tessa. "At the 5th Street Marina, just like we said."

Phillip's fingers flew over the keyboard, then he sat back, brushed his hair off his forehead. "Damn. You have to be a member, log in with a password to look at the schedule or make reservations." He cut his gaze to Zaire. "What do you want to do?"

"It's a computer program with reservation dates and availability like a hotel booking. Even if we joined, it could be weeks before we could get on board."

Phillip scrolled back to the header, noted the exact address. "I say we just go to the leasing office. San Diego's not that far. If we leave now, we can get there in a couple of hours, traffic allowing."

"Wait," Lexi said. "Shouldn't we call the police or something?"

"Based on what?" Phillip said. "My son had a vision?"

"He's right," his father told Lexi. "And if they're caught up in what we think, there'll be layers of protection." Then his hand came down on Jamal's shoulder. "Get your stuff together. We're going to get her ourselves."

Zoey paced the dressing room, watching the door. There were only five minutes left of intermission. Her stomach clenched into a tight knot that wouldn't let go. Where was Fiona?

Since Flora had issued her ultimatum, Zoe had been near speechless with anger, exhausted from holding back her rage. She had learned firsthand what Kiki had warned them about. Flora expected her to do exactly the thing she'd run away from home to avoid. And unless they found a way off this boat before the show was over, she'd be facing off with Rhalston.

"Don't look so sad, *mon petite fille*," Flora had told her. "What did you think it would be like out here in the real world? Everything handed to you on a silver platter without paying the price?"

Flora had grabbed Zoey's chin between her fingers so hard, it was all Zoey could do not to cry out. "No ma'am," she'd said through gritted teeth.

Zoey didn't know what was colder, the frigid air conditioning in the dressing room or the icy coldness of Flora's eyes. How had she not seen that before? That dancer's grace she had glimpsed the night she'd first laid eyes on Flora was gone. Maybe Zoey had only imagined it. Somewhere along the line, that grace had been compromised, Zoey thought. Damaged, and now Flora was taking out her pain on the girls.

She glared at Zoey, until, biting her bottom lip, Zoey turned away, lifted her leg to the barre, and leaned into a stretch, ignoring Flora until she flounced out of the dressing room.

Relieved to have a private moment, Zoey stretched and *piléd*, watching the clock.

Two minutes left of intermission. No Fiona.

Zoey's heart shrank into a tiny cold ball. A rack of chills raced up her arms, as she pictured Fiona on the floor, bloody and injured like Kiki.

Fiona, where are you? There was only a minute left. She couldn't go back on that stage without knowing she was alright. Her hand went instinctively to her necklace and the Zenobia coin, barely daring to breathe. She squeezed her eyes shut, and whispered, "Where are you my brother? What should I do?"

Finally, the hairs raised on the back of her neck, and an image began to take shape. *Oh my gosh! It's working.* She closed her eyes tight.

They were... together! Children, not more than five years old, holding hands inside a compound surrounded by walls of stone. In the near distance behind her, water fell musically like the trickle of a fountain, lending a sense of serenity and hope to the scene. Wait. What was this? Her visions always foretold the future, never took her to the past. But here they were, together in a landscape right out of her history lessons.

A tall woman whose hair was twisted in heavily braided strands, strode toward them and leveled her gaze on theirs. Zoey felt a rush of warmth, power, and... love, like she had never experienced in her life. Before she could respond, the woman waved an arm in a circle above her head until a whip of bright blue light began to chase her hand. It grew in brightness and intensity as she spun it out, until it was nearly as wide as her arms. And then, like pitching a ball, she cast it toward them.

The rush of blue light circled them now, brighter, faster, like a serpent chasing its tail. Zoey tried to follow it with her eyes, but it was spinning so fast she couldn't keep up. It made her dizzy, it made her laugh with the joy of it, laugh until she felt like flying...

The woman was chanting something, but Zoey couldn't hear the words. The blue lightening crackled sparked around their heads.

Then, as suddenly as it started, the woman looked toward the gate, and the lightening vanished.

The ground beneath their feet began to vibrate, gently at first, then building like an earthquake until a stampeding sound shattered the air. The noise was deafening. The little girl broke hands with her brother and covered her ears.

A gate at the far end of the compound exploded open and a half dozen horses thundered inside, driven by men perched on wooden carts.

What the holy hell? It was more than Zoey could handle after all she had been through.

She crushed her hands hard as she could against her ears and screamed for the vision leave her.

The door to the dressing room burst open. She spun around, her eyes flashing to Fiona's a fraction of a second before Flora pushed her friend to her knees. Hundred-dollar bills spilled out of Fiona's hands and fluttered all over the floor.

"Fiona!" Zoey cried, rushing to lift her up.

Flora pushed her away. "Leave her on the floor where she belongs," Flora snarled, stepping over the pile of bills. "She stole from me, the ungrateful little slut." She stabbed a tortured gaze to Zoey. "Stole from *us.*"

Fiona sobbed into her hands. "I didn't. I wouldn't." She slid an apologetic look at Zoey from between her fingers.

"Get up and wash your face, fix your make up," Flora ordered. "I'll deal with you after the second act."

Well, that didn't go well, Zoey thought.

The first strains of the prelude music for their opening dance started in. Flora pushed Zoey toward the door, her eyes narrowed into slits. "Remember what I told you earlier, *Miss* Zenobia." She pointed an accusing finger at Fiona, but her eyes drilled into Zoey's. "Her fate is in your hands."

Zoey cringed inside, her heart breaking for Fi. She wanted to comfort her friend, but if Zoe was to keep Flora's trust, she couldn't show any sympathy right now. She sent Fiona a look she hoped Flora would interpret as disdain, then flattened her back against the door, and sidled past her friend.

The music built and transitioned toward her cue. *You've got this*, she repeated over and over, like it would make a difference. Her dream of dancing her place into the world was already shattered. The only thing left was to take Flora down along with every other person involved in her scheme, even if Zoe had to sacrifice herself to do it.

They piled out of Zaire's Suburban at the Fifth Street Marina, Zaire, and Jamal in the lead.

"None of these yachts are big enough to be the *Josephine*," Jamal called out, hurrying to keep pace with his dad's long stride.

His father stopped, took in the situation. "He's right," he said to Phillip as he caught up. "You sure this is the right location?"

"The only one that can accommodate the larger vessels outside the military docks." He nodded toward the massive aircraft carriers anchored at North Island. He checked the GPS on his phone. "Judging by this picture--no telling when it was taken--the *Josephine* should be down at the far end with the other larger vessels," Phillip said, moving ahead.

Jamal hurried along the cement docks, anticipation gathering at the top of his lungs. If he was right, he was within minutes of coming face to face with his sister. Would she recognize him? Would she accept him? Was it all in his head? Was he too late? There was only one way to find out.

Ahead, was an iron gate preventing them from going any further down the private dock. His father stood outside a building next to it. Marina reception offices on one side, and private bath and shower facilities on the other, along with other commercial services. His father studied a huge map. Jamal moved in closer to take a look.

"Can I help you?" A woman with grey-blonde hair, dressed in a navy blazer, white pleated skirt, and comfortable shoes presented her hand and a broad, marketing smile.

His father straightened, the familiar deep crease settling between his brows, a man not used to asking for help.

His mother caught up. "Why, yes, I hope so. We're looking for the *Josephine.*"

The woman looked them up and down, sizing them up. She reminded Jamal of the last teacher he'd had before his dad put him on home school so they could travel. Her first answer was always *no.*

Lexi headed her off like she could read his mind. "We've been thinking of chartering her for an extended cruise and the online site, well, we just wanted to see her for ourselves before we committed our personal contact information. You understand."

"Extended?"

"Two months, maybe three," she winged it, floating a dream proposal. Jamal imagined dollar signs clicking through the woman's eyes.

Her smile returned and she extended her hand. "Won-der-ful. I'm Elizabeth Welcome, you know, like Welcome home? I manage the leasing office here. If you'll just step inside." She indicated the door to the office.

Lexi took her hand and gave it a polite pump. "Good to meet you Elizabeth."

His father stepped forward, impatience pinching the corners of his mouth. "Actually, we're in a bit of a hurry. We have another cruise to board. If you could just point us in the Josephine's direction for now..."

The woman frowned, her stern teacher face returning. She stepped away from the door. She scrutinized his father in a way that made Jamal proud and nervous at the same time. Zaire was taller than most men, darkly handsome, and when he pushed the trills of his Ethiopian accent, he often caught people off guard. In his own country, people deferred. Here in the US, however, that haughty, proper English bearing could sometimes make people nervous.

This woman was one of the nervous ones. She fiddled with the collar of her shirt. "Well, I would, but she's not here at the moment. She isn't due back until Sunday afternoon. It's a private landing. You're not allowed to..."

Jamal moaned. His patience was pulled piano-string tight. "Dad. No. We can't wait for that."

His dad pulled him close, searched his eyes a long moment, then he pulled out his phone, his no-nonsense gaze pinning the leasing agent in place. "I'm calling the Coast Guard."

"The coast guard?" She huffed out a nervous laugh. "What for?"

Jamal pushed forward, "There's girls in trouble on that vessel." His dad brought his hand down on his shoulders before he could get right in her face.

"Why that's absurd." The woman's face turned red as a lobster. She stepped to the office door, her welcome smile sliding into a scowl. "You have no evidence of anything of the kind."

"Don't need evidence," Phillip spoke up using his Colombo voice. He strolled forward with Tessa at his side like they were heading to a picnic.

The woman's hand went to her mouth. She stalked inside and scooped her phone off her desk. "You people need to leave here at once, or I'll call the police."

His dad stood his ground. "Please do. But, I strongly advise you not to call the *Josephine*." He raised a brow at her the way he did when he commanded a room in one of his board meetings. "The Coast Guard doesn't need a warrant to search a vessel, and if your phone records show you tried to warn them, that might not look good on you."

She slowly lowered her phone, sent him a skeptical look. "How do you know they don't need a warrant?"

His dad had navigated the high seas long enough to know the rules. And Phillip backed him up. He raised his own phone and read: "Title 14 section 89 of the United States Code. The U.S. Coast Guard can inquire, inspect, search, seize, and arrest if it comes to it, even if the vessel is in dry dock." He lowered his phone. "Not to mention the fact that Captain Nagatu here is a close personal friend of the local unit's base commander."

Jamal was unaware of no such thing but he wasn't about to contest it now while they had the woman off balance.

"As their booking agent," his father went on, "I'm sure the Coast Guard wouldn't mind searching your office as well."

Her mouth puckered a moment before she grabbed her purse and a shopping bag from behind a desk, then marched out the door and down the dock.

"Right," Zaire said, nodding to Phillip. "Make the call."

The dance was sensual, bordering on erotic; designed, Zoey realized now, as a prelude to what had been promised the men at the Salon. Trained to focus her gaze over the heads of the audience, it wasn't until she finished her first number that she let her gaze slip to the front row.

He was there. His cold, grey gaze met hers from only a few feet away. Sitting forward, a drink in one hand and a lit cigar in the other, he was practically drooling on the stage. The thought that to see her dance could produce that predatory stare made her stomach lurch.

She spun away, a move that wasn't in the dance, but she couldn't shake the feeling his eyes were on her, devouring her, clawing for her, claiming her. It was all she could do not to leap off the stage, run down the aisle, and out of the salon. But then what would she do? Jump overboard? Because that would be her only option if she crossed Flora right now.

Dance like your life depends on it because it probably does.

She forced her gaze up, up to the exit sign focal point she'd established in rehearsal, taking advantage of the last moments of privacy she'd have before lust and greed robbed her of herself.

The end of the dance left her in a provocative pose that heated her cheeks when the men in the audience shouted their response. They may be respectable men of the world, but here in his salon, they were nothing but dogs.

She was off the stage and running for the dressing room before the final curtain hit the floor.

She burst into the dressing room expecting to see Fiona. Instead, Flora stood in front of a mirrored dressing table with a bouquet of red roses in one arm and a wardrobe bag in the other.

For the first time in her life, the fragrance of roses made Zoey's stomach clench. She didn't have to ask where they came from.

Her disgust must have showed on her face because Flora sent her a stiff smile and dropped the roses on the makeup table. "Learn to appreciate what you get from this, Zoey. Few people on earth are offered such luxury."

She bit back her reply. How is it luxury when you have no control over your own body? Your future? Your friends?

Instead, she simply glared at the woman. "Where's Fiona?"

"Never mind Fiona. She made a bad choice and now she's dealing with the consequences. Just worry about doing your job if you want to keep it. Rhalston will be waiting in his suite. Go to your room, shower, change into this." She pushed the wardrobe bag at her. A costume photo hung at the hook. A dark-skinned girl dressed like a Nubian queen.

Disgust knotted Zoey throat at the thought that a man planned to use her for his own fantasy. If it wasn't for Kiki and Fiona's lives in the balance, she would crush him before she'd let that happen.

"Take it," Flora said, impatiently. "Chantal will take you to him in a half hour." She opened the dressing room door. "Well? What are you waiting for? *Go!* The sooner you get this over with, the sooner you can get back to your precious Fi."

Zoey stood her ground a moment longer, her gaze fixed on Flora's until she saw tiny lines of doubt crease the corners of her eyes.

Slinging the garment bag over her shoulder more casually than she actually felt, she couldn't resist bumping Flora's shoulder aside as she strode out the door. She had no idea how she would handle the next hour with Rhalston, but one thing she knew for certain: Flora would spend it wondering whether or not Zoe would do as she was told.

In her private suite, Zoey stood in front of the full-length mirror and smoothed silky gold lame fabric over her hips. The gown's deep cut neckline dipped low, showcasing the Zenobia coin where it rested between the swell of her breasts. Lapis, coral, and gold-tone beads were braided into a thick hair piece she'd pinned at the crown of her head, then pulled the rest forward to cascade over her bare shoulder.

More beads embroidered in an intricate pattern about the dress's hipline gave the appearance of a bejeweled belt. She carefully tied the halter top in a half bow at the nape of her neck as shown in the photo on the garment bag. Then, she laced the blue satin espadrilles up her calves. In any other circumstance, she would have loved them.

She turned her back to the mirror and looked over her shoulder. The low cut back left her bare well below her waist. Side slits showed leg up to her hips as she walked. The clingy fabric, and the way it draped over her skin left little to the imagination. The description said: No underwear. If she didn't remove her panties now, Chantal would instruct her to do so when she arrived, so she slipped hers off.

She turned back around, taking it all in. Flora certainly knew how to package her product. One tug at the tie at her neck and the gown would slide off her body like melting gold.

She steeled herself against a rack of chills. She wouldn't let things get that far if she could help it. Resigned, she ran glossy red lipstick over her mouth and faked a smile.

"That could use some work," she mumbled, her fingers going once more to the necklace for support.

"My brother if you hear me, now would be a good time to let me know." She closed her eyes and breathed in, listening to her heartbeat as precious moments ticked by.

Nothing.

The crushing weight of loss grew heavy in her chest. Where was he? Why in the darkest moment of her life, did he not hear her call? She squeezed her eyes shut.

She was holding on tighter, fearing the *sight* had abandoned her, when an odd jolt of static shot through her fingers, and words began to swirl around in her head. Unintelligible at first, then stronger, clearer, insistent: *Just a little longer, Roshana. Hold on just a little longer.*

Was it him? Was he here?

She spun around, but instead of seeing him, the motion set her off balance. The walls of her suite began to move. Gold lame fabric sailed out from her hips as she spun faster and faster until the room around her blurred. She squeezed her eyes shut against the dizzying spin. Make it stop. *Make. It. Stop!*

And, as if on command. It did!

She gasped, not knowing which way was up, arms pressed away from her to find anything stable. When she opened her eyes, she wasn't in her suite. In fact, if what she was seeing was true, she wasn't on the yacht. She was back in the place she had been with her brother, only this time she saw through the eyes the warrior queen.

*　　*　　*

Her husband stood beside her, his arm gripping her waist tight, holding her in place at his side as her children were loaded on carts to be carried away.

Her heart ached. She panicked. She had made a terrible mistake, but it was too late. As the gates closed behind them, she had another vision that would haunt her to the end of her days. The sounds of a storm, converging currents, and the terrifying groan of timbers being pulled apart assaulted her. She covered her ears and cried out as she watched what could only be the ship carrying her children overwhelmed by a storm. "No," she cried out as it dipped, then circled, then sank to the bottom of the great sea.

*　　*　　*

Footsteps sounded down the hall outside her door. A loud knock made her jump inside her skin. She couldn't get the images out of her head. *My god. My god! Zenobia had foreseen her children's ship sink into the sea? Zoe's heart pinched at the thought of the pain she must have endured.* She gulped air, willing her heartbeat to settle.

The knock came again, bringing her fully into the present. It had to be Chantal.

"Zoey. Open this door. We have to go. Now! Don't make this any harder than it has to be."

Zoey straightened, pulled herself together, leaning into the mirror a moment to fix a smudge of mascara under her eye.

"I'm coming," she called out, willing herself to lift her chin. *Get a grip, girl.* She. Or someone who felt like it could have been her in another lifetime, had suffered things much worse than what Flora had planned for her now. *Just hold on a little longer, Roshana. Zoe. Just hold on a little longer.*

He was shorter than she imagined when she'd first seen him. His hands were meaty and thick, and those eyes. It wasn't that they were light in color, it was that lacked any color at all. Right now, his gaze slid from her hair to her eyes, to her mouth like he wanted to eat her for dessert. Then his gaze slid down her chest to focus on her gold pendant, the pupils of his eyes expanded to appear like polished black stones.

Uncertainty fluttered its wings insider her chest. Whatever made her think she could stand up to this man?

Kiki and Fiona's lives depend on you, that's what, she told herself.

She pulled herself up to stand hipshot, hand on hip, and faked her best showgirl smile. "Good evening, Mr. Rhalston," she said, trilling her accent as instructed.

Chantal gave her a little push from behind. "I'll come and get you in an hour," she said, her eyes shifting to Ralston's, as if in reminder.

He bowed his head, opened the door all the way, and swept his hand wide for Zoey to enter his suite.

She bit her bottom lip, taking it all in. The executive suite occupied the entire stern of the vessel on the top level; a sunken sitting area faced an expansive, private deck boasting a bar, a hot tub, and a massive round bed, at the center, piled with pillows. A cheesy cover of a Michael Bublé song played over the scene. Her stomach felt like she was going to heave up her dinner. She breathed in through her nose to head off the wave of nausea.

Her saving grace was the Milky Way spreading its path across the night sky. Like the dance, it was something to focus on. Not many people got to see it this way, unobstructed by city lights or coastal fog. She understood now what Flora meant when she said she should appreciate the benefits of accepting this lifestyle. Lavish clothes, world travel, the ultimate in private luxury. A person could get used to this lifestyle if they were willing to pay the price.

She didn't want or need this gaudy, over-done lifestyle. She had seen the same Milky Way lying flat on her back holding hands with Shuda in her family's okra patch. A tear pushed at the corner of her eye. Truly, there was not enough champagne or silk dresses in all the world to make up for losing her friend.

She stepped to the railing, rested her hands there, and thought: How long had Flora been on the menu before she was relegated to setting younger women up for this? What if she accepted the role of *fille de jour*? Would it be worth it?

She nipped a tear with her knuckle, braced her hands on the railing, then flinched at the sound of a cork popping behind her. There was the sound of bubbly liquid being poured into glasses, then Rhalston's footsteps approached.

"You're named after a Queen, did you know that?" His breath was warm against her bare shoulder. Zoey lifted her chin. *If he only knew.* If Zoey could believe her visions, she was a direct descendent of the Queen. The certain knowledge flooded her with confidence. *Fille de jour my ass.*

A couple of inches taller than the man, Zoey looked down on him now. He might be the master of this yacht but take away the fancy suit and the gold rings, he was no different than her cousin. A bully dog forcing himself on someone he perceived to be naive and weak. She would let him think that until she let him get close enough, then she'd slam her knee into his groin. She took the champagne flute and sipped, staring him down the way she'd done with Flora.

He wasn't deterred. It was more like he enjoyed the challenge. Those grey eyes locked on hers and did not let go. She stiffened when his fingers caressed the bare skin at her low back, then trailed up her spine to the tie at her nape. She needed him in front of her.

She turned demurely out of his grasp and faced him, one hand holding the champagne flute aloft like an *ingénue* in a movie, the other held on to the coin.

"She was a warrior Queen, did you know that?" she asked, mocking his tone. "Nearly conquered half the Roman Empire."

Doubt shadowed his brow, and she felt a definite shift of power in that moment. Zenobia's blood heated in her veins.

"Ah, I see you are nervous," he said, "There's no hurry my dear. Drink your champagne."

Nervous. Maybe. But it worked in her favor. Heightened her senses. She sent him a demure smile.

He took a step back, refilled her glass and, still admiring her body, crooned, "There are chocolates here, too. Did you see?" He offered a tray of sweets, white chocolate dipped strawberries, cannoli.

Chocolates? Cannoli? Yes. Anything to delay. Delay. Delay. She sipped more champagne, letting the bubbles tickle her throat.

He stood patiently by as she selected a strawberry from the tray, but when she lifted it to her lips and her eyes met his, he lost his restraint. In one swift move, he closed the distance between them, lifted his hand to the back of her neck, and pulled the tie at her nape, catching her completely off guard.

The dress melted off of her, sliding over her breasts, her hips, then pooling at her feet. She stood, bare skinned and quivering before him now, wearing nothing but the blue satin espadrilles and the Zenobia coin necklace. Every cell in her body wanted to scream and run away, but she couldn't turn her back on him. Not now. Not if she wanted to take him down.

He put down his glass, dragged his tongue slowly over his bottom lip, and reached out toward her breast.

Now-or-never, now-or-never. She cocked her knee, grasping the necklace tight. It was now, or never. The moment her knee connected with his body, a blue light exploded around them, seeming to draw its power from her intent. It knocked him across the deck. But he wasn't down. Not yet. Armed with a power she had no idea she possessed, she stalked toward him, ignoring her nakedness, and cocked a fist. "This is the last time you'll take advantage of a young girl again." In another flash of blue flame, she drew back, then punched him straight in the chest, driving him to the railing. He raised his arms, trying to protect his face, but with her newfound strength, she rounded on him again with a blazing upper cut that lifted his body up and over the railing. He tumbled backward over the side, arms flailing, his scream cut short by a splash as he hit the water below.

She gasped and covered her eyes a moment. Did that really happen? Peeking between her fingers, she saw that it was so. The pale eyed monster had gone overboard, and in his place, a vortex of blue lightening spun itself into a tight ball, hung there a moment as if to take a bow, then vanished like a shooting star burning itself out on the horizon.

She let go of the necklace and screamed until every ounce of strength left her body. She melted to her knees and rolled to her back, exhausted.

There was a perfect silence now. The Milky Way still cut its path across the sky and she marveled at the thought that Zenobia and her children probably witnessed the same view thousands of years ago. The thought soothed her a moment before the blackness closed in.

She was shaking all over when red and blue light stabbed the night sky and strobed across the deck. The silence gave way to a low engine rumble somewhere nearby. What was this? Disoriented, she rolled over and was pushing to her knees to stand when she heard footsteps behind her.

"Roshana?"

A fresh jolt of shock shot through her chest. She pulled herself up at the railing, covered her breasts with her hands, and turned to see a uniformed woman standing in the sunken seating area. Stepping slowly through the space, she pulled the duvet off the massive bed. "You're okay," she said gently, inching closer. "I'm with the Coast Guard. Let's cover you up, okay?"

She closed the final distance between them and carefully draped the duvet over Zoey's shoulders. *The coast guard? But, how?* She gathered the warmth around her shoulders, not sure she could make herself speak through her chattering jaws. "How... How do you know my name?"

The woman gathered her under her arm and guided her off the deck and into the cabin. She lowered her down on the sofa. "Your family is at the dock."

"My family?" Zoey dragged in a breath, incredulous. What on earth was this woman talking about. Her aunt? Her cousin? After all she'd been through? All she'd risked getting away, they'd found her? This couldn't be happening. Her fleeting moment of relief turn to shattered disappointment. They were the last people she wanted to see.

"Your brother, Jamal, and your parents are on shore. You'll be back home soon. Don't worry."

"Worry?" Zoey blinked at the officer. Had she heard right? Her brother? The boy who had been in her dreams her entire life? Her teeth began to chatter again. And her parents? What on earth did she mean, her parents?

Then another cold jolt struck through her. "Where's Fiona and Kiki? Are they all right?"

The woman held up a finger, spoke into her radio. "Got her. Everyone's accounted for." Then to Zoey she said, "Your friends have been offloaded to the coast guard ship, along with all the other girls. Fiona told us where to find you."

Relief swept over her, she let out a long breath. The chattering was intermittent now, interrupted by short sobs she tried to hold back. She had faced the enemy and she had survived. They all had. Except, the silver-eyed man. The memory of his wail as he pitched overboard crashed in. They'd been fighting, struggling, when a flash of blue light took over, drove her fury at Rhalston's body. She wasn't sure exactly what happened but one thing was sure, that awful man was gone when she came to.

"That man. Rhalston? He tried to... I fought him and... " Tears spilled down her cheeks. "I think... I think I killed him."

The officer shook her head. "No, honey. You didn't kill him. We have him in custody. He was picked up by some crew members in a Zodiac launch trying to escape the vessel." Her gaze combed over the deck outside. "Was there a fire?"

Zoey let out a sigh of relief. But, a fire? She went to the sliding doors, gazed out over the deck and closed her eyes a moment, remembered the blue lightening swirling around them, smashing into him like fists. There was no point in telling the officer, she wouldn't believe her if she did. "No," she said at last. "At least I... don't think so. I don't remember."

The woman stared at her incredulously. "He had severe burns over his face and upper body. Are you sure?"

A wave of shame tightened her chest, until she remembered the look in his eyes right before he reached for her. Those colorless eyes said it all. She was nothing to him. Just something to play with and have his way. Something to control, ruin, then throw away. She gripped the necklace in her fist and held it close to her heart. "I don't know. Like I said," she murmured, lifting her gaze to the officer. "We fought, I fell, and that's... all I remember."

Zoey stood on the transom of the Salacia, trying not to hyperventilate as she gazed into the deep blue water below, her brother by her side. He leaned in and shoulder bumped her. "So, are you ready?"

She closed her eyes, smiled, and shook her head, her heart beating hard, like a trapped seagull in her chest.

Her father's voice came from behind her. "It's okay, Zoey. Take a step back and relax a minute. We're in no hurry."

Relieved, she stepped away from the edge and leaned against the railing, letting the events of the last few weeks sift through her mind.

In just a few short weeks Jamal had taught her to snorkel which was no small task since she barely knew how to swim. Next came scuba lessons and getting certified in a diving pool. All that, while everything else was going on.

They'd spent hours sitting on the seawall at the Grand Canal in front of Lexi's home on Balboa Island getting to know each other. Zoey had shared her passion for dance, her dreams of dancing on the world's most famous stages. Jamal was nothing if not passionate about saving the coral reefs. He wanted her to share that passion with him.

It had been six weeks since the coast guard had boarded the *Josephine* and she met her biological mother and father for the first time and reclaimed her United States citizenship. It hadn't been as easy for Fiona and Kiki who were foreign born. But with Phillip and Tessa's help, they had been classified as victims, not criminals or prostitutes in the *Josephine* affair, which was a good first step. They had secured T Visas, and sponsored by Tessa and Phillip, were housed with them on Balboa Island, right next door to Zoe. The rest of the girls were being housed in San Diego with Immigration Services who were working on finding their relatives overseas.

Yesterday, Phillip received word from the Justice Department that Rhalston had been released from the U.C. Irvine Medical Center Burn Center into the custody of the Federal Marshall. Zoey received the news with relief. As much as the man deserved to be punished for what he'd done, she didn't want to have his death on her conscience for the rest of her life. He would see the scars of his crimes every time he looked in a mirror for the rest of his.

They would all have to testify to the Justice Department eventually, a fact that made her stomach churn whenever she thought about it. If it were up to her, she never wanted to see Flora again. But the girls' testimony would be key to getting indictments against Flora, Chantal, Angelica, and the owners of the *Josephine*. Phillip had learned that the leasing agent who had gotten immunity for her testimony, said the *Josephine* had been involved in similar activity for several years.

Despite all they had done to make her feel welcome, Zoey was still having difficulty thinking of Zaire and Alexis as Mom and Dad. Believing her parents had abandoned her to live in a terrible situation had become so much a part of the fabric of her being, she was finding it hard to replace the old dialogs running in her head. She had a lot to process. Her heart wanted the freedom of forgiveness, but her body still flinched when a door opened behind her, suspected ulterior motives when there was clearly only care and concern.

She kept a tight rein on her heart, not because she didn't want to let them in, but because she did. Tessa, a constant companion who had promised to teach her how to cast gold granules into jewelry, assured her that her heart would open more in time. Zoey wanted to believe her.

They were all a little off balance. After all, Zai and Lexi had only learned what had happened to their children recently themselves. Lexi had admitted to her only yesterday how she was still coming to terms with the fact that the young man she thought had abandoned her all those years ago, had not known anything about her pregnancy, or the *adoptions*.

She could see in their eyes, their reunion had been the best thing to ever happen to them. There were wedding plans in their future.

And who could complain about having her own room on the top floor of a gorgeous home overlooking the Grand Canal with her best friends right next door? It was like Zoey fallen into a dream. The fact that her actual father was an international hospitality mogul worth billions was so far out of the realm of her reality she had pushed that knowledge completely off her radar. For now, he was just the guy who shared a breakfast table with her in the morning and took her out to meet her mother for chowder down on the bay. He had, after all, promised her a trip back to Botswana to see her precious Shuda. Apparently, Zaire owned a safari resort near the Chobi river, fancy that? And how could you not love a mother who wanted nothing more than to do everything in her power to help you reach your dreams?

It was harder to find compassion for her grandmother. She could have spared them all years of pain and suffering if she had only done the right thing fifteen years earlier. But who knew what the right thing was. Even the wrong path can sometimes lead to the right place, Lexi had reminded her. And Zoey believed that was true.

She marveled at the depth of forgiveness Lexi was willing to give, offering to let her mother live with them until… her end. It made Zoey love her mother that much more. But Althea wouldn't hear of it. She had a small home in Addis Ababa and she wanted to return there for whatever time she had left in this world, claiming that she had never felt she belonged in the States.

The most amazing thing of all the events over the last month, though, had been discovering that boy in her dreams was real. They had reached out to one another over a tenuous thread of time and space and fought their way back together.

She had to keep pinching herself to make sure she wasn't dreaming. She saw the same look of wonder in his eyes every time he looked at her. One day she would meet a boy and fall in love and make a life with him the way her mother had met and loved Zaire; but in her heart of hearts she knew, she would never, ever let herself be separated from Jamal again. They had traveled time together and that was something she could never share with another soul.

Just yesterday, she and her mother had officially applied to change her legal name. When she stepped out on stage in her first dance recital at the Center for the Performing Arts, she would be Miss Zoey Page Nagatu.

The only question in her heart was how she and Jamal would relate to the magical gift they had been given in this modern world. What had happened to Zenobia's twins, after all?

As if he could feel her thoughts, Jamal stepped up beside her, slipped his hand in hers, and leaned in so only she could hear. "One day, we'll wear the serpents and coins and we'll time travel together and discover the rest of our story."

The idea sent a shiver though her bones. He lifted a mischievous brow in a way that was becoming familiar to Zoe. "Yeah?" he prodded.

"No," she said on a laugh, releasing some of her nervous fear. "I'm happy to be living in this life right now, thank you."

She rubbed her hands together, shook out her legs, and glanced at her dad and Lexi standing behind them. Her heart filled with warmth that spread all the way to her toes. There may be vast treasures under the sea--in gold and in the natural world--but none of that would ever compare to the treasure she'd discovered right here in front of her. She had a family and she knew beyond all doubt and fears that was all the treasure she'd ever need.

"Okay, you two," her dad said, guiding her back to the edge of the transom, then checking the valves on her scuba gear one more time. "On the count of three, right? One, two, three..."

With a last glance over her shoulder to her mother, and a squeeze of Jamal's hand, she drew in a breath and stepped off into the deep blue water.

Thank you for reading The Serpent's Coil, Book 3 in my Serpent's Coil Historical Time Travel Series. For now, this is the final book in the series, but who knows, if Jamal presses his sister, he might get her to go on another time travel adventure.

Authors thrive on feedback and reviews. I would love it if you took a moment to leave a short review. At your retailer, Goodreads, or Bookbub.

For more books by Kat Drennan, snap the QR code below to go to her Amazon Author Page

About the Author

Kat Drennan writes sensual stories from the heart of the Golden State.

From the curling surf at the edge of the continent, to the granite sculptures of the Sierra Nevada; from San Francisco to Death Valley and all the way to the Mexican border and beyond, California's unique landscape and colorful, dramatic history step forward as characters in each of her novels.

She is an alumna of the Squaw Valley Community of Writers, as well as a member of Romance Writers of America, and past Secretary of the Contemporary Romance Writers Chapter of RWA.

Based in Ojai, California, Kat loves the beach, a challenging bike ride, cooking with a friend, and watching her two granddaughters grow.

She loves to hear from her readers. You can follow her at www.katdrennanbooks.com, sign up for her newsletter to find out about new releases, or follow her Facebook page to hear about new releases, freebies, and other promotions.